Treasure Beyond Time

By Darlia Sawyer

Copyright © 2021
Written by: Darlia Sawyer
Published by: Forget Me Not Romances, a division of Winged Publications.

This book is a work of fiction. Names, characters, places, and incidents are the product of the author's imagination and are used fictitiously. Any resemblance to actual events, locales, or persons, living or dead, is coincidental.

All rights reserved.

ISBN: 979-8-3493-0400-2

Special thanks to my family for their support.

My husband, Ken, for his hours of content editing. He makes sure I keep everything real and tie up all loose ends. I couldn't do it without him.

My son, Nick, for the cover design and putting his major in graphic design to work.

My sister, Misty, for coming up with the title for it.

My mom, Mary, for reading through it and giving suggestions.

My sister, Holly, for reading through it and giving suggestions.

My Word Weavers writing group for their helpful critiques and Templa for helping with the back blurb.

And of course my publisher, Cynthia, for her understanding and help.

Chapter One

"Your attention, please. Olivia Hanson. Olivia Hanson. Come to the counter at Gate 34." Olivia recognized her name as it blared over the intercom system at Orlando International Airport.

She turned around and headed back to her gate. *Why did they want to see her? Had she done something wrong?* Her stomach did flip-flops as she walked up to the desk. "Hi, I'm Olivia Hanson. I heard my name being paged."

"Can I look at your identification, please?" the airport attendant asked.

Olivia reached into her purse and pulled out her driver's license.

"Thank you, Miss Hanson. Did you leave this bag under your seat?"

Oliva took the backpack from the young man. "Thank you so much! I can't believe I forgot it. My trip would've been ruined if you hadn't noticed it."

"We had to search inside to ensure there we no

bombs," he said with a wink and smile. "Are you going on a treasure-hunting trip? I couldn't help but see the books on sunken ships in Florida among the items in your pack."

"I am. I've been looking forward to this trip my whole life."

"Well, enjoy your time in Florida, Miss Hanson. I hope you discover a treasure worth millions."

Olivia smiled. "Thank you, sir. Thanks again for finding my bag."

The airport attendant nodded and motioned the next person to move to the counter.

Olivia walked through the airport terminal using the people movers to get her to the tram. It was the only way to the main concourse. She hopped on as it was ready to depart, then sat in an empty bench seat. She glanced out the window at the palm trees swaying in the wind under the intense Florida sun.

She disembarked when it stopped and walked to the airport baggage claim. She waited for her hot pink suitcase with glittery hearts in various bright colors to come out on the conveyor belt. She'd wanted to make sure she could tell it apart from everyone else's. There was no need for worry as when it came out, all the little girls were saying they needed one like hers.

Olivia had given up hope of this adventure ever happening. Fortunately, she found this team of treasure hunters online who took ordinary people out on their searches. At fifteen she had decided one day she would look for lost riches. It had only taken twenty more years to come to fruition.

She wheeled her luggage out the airport concourse doors. A few people stood around talking. Huge round cement containers of multicolored flowers bordered the walkway outside. Sweat formed on her forehead from the stifling humidity. Coming from a dry climate near the Rocky Mountains of Colorado, she'd not been prepared for the thick heaviness as she inhaled the moisture-laden air.

She didn't recall who was to pick her up, she thought his name was Jake. She'd been so excited to be accepted into this exploration team, the details hadn't seemed important.

Oliva rolled her suitcase over to the perfect sitting wall bordering flower beds. She sat on the edge. She should've brought a hat, as it wouldn't take long for her skin to turn bright red. Her sunglasses were buried somewhere in one of her bags.

A white van rolled up and stopped about 10 yards away from her. The side of it had *Florida Treasure Hunters* painted in pink and blue pastels, along with a treasure chest spilling coins and jewelry from its box.

A man got out holding a sign that said, Olivia Hanson.

Her ride was here. Olivia walked over to him.

"You must be Olivia Hanson?" He said.

"Yes, I am."

"Hi Olivia, I'm Jake Crowley. I'll be taking you to your hotel. We'll be getting started early tomorrow, so you should turn in early tonight. The days are long." He took Olivia's bags and loaded them into the van.

Olivia got in and closed the passenger door. She had to admit her stomach had yet to settle down. She'd never done anything close to this. Not only flying to Florida by herself, but joining a group of people from around the country who were interested in discovering lost treasure.

Jake opened the door and hopped in. "Where you from?"

Olivia jumped.

"Didn't mean to startle you." Jake tried not to laugh.

"Sorry, guess I was absorbed in my thoughts. I'm from Colorado."

"You're far from home. Ever been here before?" Jake turned off the airport loop and onto SR 528 toward the east coast of Florida.

"No, sadly. I haven't been to any other states. This will be my first time seeing the ocean. Have you always lived in Florida?" Olivia looked out the side window. Trees lined the freeway, making it tough to see anything beyond them.

"Yes. I've lived here all my life. I travel often but I always come home. Florida's a great place to live and search for treasure. A lot of ships have sunk off our coast. We've found some gold coins over the years along the beach.

We are close to identifying the wreckage of one of the Spanish Treasure ships. At least we think so. We managed to obtain a permit for an area we think contains the wreckage of this ship. Are you a certified diver, Olivia?"

"Nope, never got my certification. I've only dived in lakes and pools. I don't have ocean experience. I hope with the guidance of your team, I can make some shallow dives. I'd like to get certified one day." Olivia unzipped her purse and took out her chapstick.

"I'm glad you have a realistic expectation of how this goes. There will be a beach team and a diving party. Most of the time you'll be using metal detectors on the sand. If you come again, be here a few days early and we can get you certified. The good thing for you is we'll be in water 20 to 30 feet deep just off the coast and it's not illegal to dive without a certification. There are no 'scuba police' to put you in prison. It shouldn't be a problem for you to do a couple of dives if the ocean's not too rough. Most of the time on the boat is spent watching the divers.

You should like your hotel, it's in one of the nicest areas along Melbourne Beach. Well, I think so. The name is the Ocean Front Hotel. You can step right out the back doors of the lobby and be on the sand in a few steps. Did you need to stop anywhere first?" Jake turned and smiled at Olivia as he took an off-ramp onto highway A1A along the coast.

Their eyes met, and Olivia returned his smile. *He has dimples and is kinda cute.*

"I'd rather go straight to the hotel. It's been a long day. I'll order room service and go to sleep or at least attempt to. You did say we'd be getting an early start." Olivia covered a yawn with her hand.

"Sounds good." Jake signaled and turned into the hotel parking lot.

"Let me grab your bags while you check-in," he opened his door and got out.

The multi-story hotel was in an older but remodeled section of Melbourne Beach, right on the ocean. She got out of the van and heard the crashing of the waves in the distance. The smell of saltwater saturated the air. She followed Jake as he wheeled her suitcases into the lobby. He made quite the entrance with the hot pink suitcase.

"I'll be here at 7:30 sharp to pick you up with the rest of the group. Have a pleasant night." Jake left her bag by the front desk.

Olivia checked in and found her room. She set her

backpack and purse on the bed and rolled her suitcase into a corner. She opened the sliding glass doors and walked out onto a balcony that overlooked the ocean. She stepped to the railing and stood in awe.

Below her, white sand stretched as far as she looked in both directions. In front of her, the florescent green ocean glistened to the horizon. The sound of waves breaking along the shoreline and a gentle breeze blowing through her hair mixed with the smell of the sea air and permeated her senses. Had she found paradise?

She wanted to run along the water's edge and feel the sand between her toes, but it would have to wait until tomorrow. As she closed the sliding glass doors and drew the drapes shut, her stomach rumbled. She hadn't eaten all day, except for the sack of peanuts she had on the plane. Time for dinner. On the nightstand, there was an information notebook that contained the menu for the seafood restaurant connected to the hotel. After looking through it, Olivia contacted room service then laid down. The bed was comfortable, not like some, where you might as well of been laying on plywood.

The pale blue and green paint complemented the beach paintings hanging on the walls. The room was furnished with a mini-frig, coffee maker, microwave, and of course a TV. Thankfully, the frig was stocked as she'd forgotten to order a drink. She pulled out a diet Coke and popped the tab. She loved the sound of bubbles fizzing in the can. *It's the small things, Olivia*, she told herself.

She wished she had someone to share this experience with. Her ex-boyfriend, Ryan, had been a significant part of her life and they'd planned on coming together, or so she assumed. Six months ago she found texts on his phone from a woman and when she confronted him he said he wanted to break up with her. He claimed the messages were innocent but realized he wasn't ready to settle down with anyone. Another failure to add to the list of guys she hoped was *The One*. How could she be so wrong at choosing *Mr. Right*? Most of her relationships hadn't lasted longer than a year.

After her parents died in a car accident ten years ago, Olivia had been alone. She'd never had any siblings, and her grandparents had been gone since she was a child. She had a few distant cousins she hadn't met and a couple of girlfriends she ate dinner with every few months. Olivia realized how void of meaningful relationships her life was.

That's why she stayed as busy as possible with teaching history at a local Denver community college, volunteering at the state historical society, writing, and her summer job as a lifeguard. Time for her was rare. As she sat on the bed staring at the décor, her loneliness hit full force. Tears she'd held at bay over the breakup with her boyfriend spilled out. *Why was life so cruel*?

A tap on the door brought Olivia back to reality. She shut off the tears, splashed water on her face, and peered through the peephole. It was room service. She let him in long enough to sit her bag of food on the table, tip and thank him, then she locked the door behind him. She took out the Styrofoam containers, then opened them. She was relieved to see a tasty dinner of salmon, brown rice with quinoa, broccoli, and a side salad with a vinaigrette. She squeezed the lemon wedge, and the juice dripped over her fish. It smelled wonderful. She buttered the warmed baguette and watched the butter melt and run over the sides. They'd included a cup of water, and for dessert

German chocolate cake with a small scoop of vanilla ice cream. The temptation was too much. She ate the dessert first.

~

Olivia exited the elevator and walked out into the hotel foyer. Five or six people were mulling around, the only noise was from the television behind the front desk. She was early. A massive chandelier hung from the vaulted blue and white Moroccan tile-covered ceiling. There were huge bay windows on the back wall providing a picturesque view of the ocean.

She searched for Jake. No trace of him. She wondered if any of the people would be going with them today. She smelled bacon and coffee and walked into a small room across from the front desk. They included a free continental breakfast, so she walked over and poured herself a cup of coffee. She snatched an apple, two slices of bacon, and a chocolate chip muffin, then sat down at an unoccupied table. A couple with young children were making waffles, they jumped up and down in anticipation of the golden yumminess awaiting them.

Jake stuck his head into the room. "Hi Olivia, you ready to leave?"

"Hi. I got here a little early and decided to get some coffee and a few goodies. Would you like anything?" Olivia threw her muffin wrapper away, shoved the bacon in her mouth, and grabbed the apple.

"No thanks, I picked something up on the way here. Everyone's in the van. The first day's always full of anticipation and apprehension. Let's go!"

Jake strode toward the lobby doors with Olivia

following. He was handsome. He had the classic surfer boy looks - golden hair, teal blue eyes, and dark tan. He must be at least six feet tall.

Everyone was settled in the van when she opened the sliding door, but thankfully, they left a vacant spot next to the exit. She didn't want to climb over anybody. She noticed a new man in the front passenger seat as Jake hopped in the driver's chair. He started talking.

"Thanks, everyone for choosing *Florida Treasure Hunters*. We appreciate your confidence in us to guide you in this adventure. Many of you have traveled a long distance. The quest for treasure along the Florida east coast has drawn lots of people. Whether along the beach or in the water just offshore, millions of dollars of coins and jewelry, and artifacts have been discovered in the last one hundred years.

If this is your first trip or just another of many, or whether we discover something of value, we guarantee you won't be disappointed. Today, we'll visit Melbourne Beach to scan for treasure using our state-of-the-art metal detectors. There have been gold coins found along these beaches.

Tomorrow, many of you will go out on one of our two treasure hunting boats and some of you who have dive experience may get to dive with our experienced crew. They will be with you every minute.

As a company, *Florida Treasure Hunters* have secured a permit for an area off the coast here. We have researched extensively, and now believe the Spanish ship, *Santisima Trinidad,* which sank during a hurricane in 1715, is just off Melbourne beach.

We will separate into two groups and search for coins across a five-mile stretch of beach near this permitted area. After, there will be a picnic lunch served of red snapper, rice, and assorted veggies. Then to cap off the day we'll have a fresh crab boil over an open fire and some delicious sweets. So, buckle up, our destination is about eight minutes south of where we are."

~

Olivia ran ahead of the people in her group. She made her way to the water's edge and slipped off her sandals. A breaking wave just offshore sent seawater over her feet and shins at a rate rapid enough to splash her upper body too. The reseeding pull of the ocean dragged her with it as it flowed back out to sea. Her feet were sunk into the sand a couple of inches. She stayed in the same spot as another wave surged in and then out. She laughed as she mentally crossed an item off her bucket list.

"Is the Colorado girl enjoying her first time at the beach?"

Olivia turned to see Jake walking toward her.

"I am. It's everything I imagined and more." Olivia turned back toward the ocean.

"I can't imagine what it must be like seeing it for the first time. I grew up going to the beach, so I take it for granted. I hate to disturb your special moment, but we're about to start instructing everyone on the operation of the metal detectors. So come on over." Jake grinned, his dimples showing again.

"Of course. I'm so sorry. Here I was thinking of what I wished to do and not considering the group. Let me put my sandals back on and I'll be right over." Olivia walked out of the water and tried to brush the sand off her feet.

"Good luck with that." Jake laughed as he sauntered back to the group.

I'm showing my lack of experience in all things beach and ocean-related. Olivia shoved her feet into the sandals. As she made her way toward the group, her wet feet slid around on the insoles of the now sand-crusted sandals, making squeaky noises as she stepped.

"Okay, I assume we're all here now. Let's introduce ourselves and tell a little about what brought us here." The guy who'd been sitting in the passenger seat started talking again.

"Hi everybody, my name is David Townsend, and I am co-owner of *Florida Treasure Hunters* along with Jake Crowley and Mike Snow. Our team has been searching for lost ships all over the world for ten years now, but our focus has been on the coastlines here. We've had some good luck, but many more busts.

The last couple of years we've been concentrating on the 1715 Spanish Treasure Fleet, all of which sank off the east coast here during a hurricane. Many more men perished than survived, but it's believed that around 1100 did survive.

These ships are presumed to be strewn along what is called the Treasure Coast of Florida. The area encompasses Sebastian Inlet, then south to the town of Jupiter. Not every boat from the fleet has been found, although it has been extensively explored. We hope we have located the wreckage of the *Santisima Trinidad.* It's one of the two ships not found. This will be an exciting adventure. We hope to find some coins or artifacts or better yet, the major discovery of this missing ship."

The aroma of seafood whiffed by her nose, causing her eyes to glance towards the dunes. A catering company was setting up tables and chairs, and prepping for dinner. Her stomach rumbled. Olivia's skin gleamed red when she glanced down at her arms. She'd been so caught up in her pursuit for the treasure she'd neglected to reapply her sunscreen. Looked like a stop at Walmart later to buy some Aloe would be in order.

Olivia made her way toward the food, as others were doing. Three large gas grills had been fired up, two grilling fish and veggies. The other grill cooking rice and frying hushpuppies.

She hadn't communicated with anyone today. Olivia had been listening to the history of the 1715 treasure fleet, learning the proper technique of using the metal detectors and hoping she'd find some gold coins. She learned it was better to scan for treasure during high wave action or after a storm or hurricane. The storms caused erosion and sand movement, opening up areas that before were a foot or so buried. Olivia hadn't found anything of value but did find some current U.S. coins and a few buried soda cans.

No one in either group discovered anything of great value. One man dug up an old fishing knife someone must have left behind. It had been a fun day, hearing the excitement from everyone as their metal detectors hit on something under the sand. The tales of their discoveries went on and on as they told how they found many interesting items.

Throughout the day, she'd let her mind drift to what life must have been like in 1715. How it had been remarkable anyone had survived the hurricanes. She thought about what they must have endured after the storm. A shiver ran down her back as she imagined some of the dangers. One thing was certain, they were accustomed to the unknown as they were at sea for weeks and sometimes months. They were at the mercy of a vast and powerful ocean full of so many variables. She wondered how they found the courage to board those ships that went in pursuit of new lands. *Could she have done the same?*

"How'd your day go?" Jake startled her.

Olivia smiled. "It was a lot of fun. I'm glad I came."

"I'm glad. Odds are not in favor of locating any lost treasure, but the hope is we will. It's the reason we continue and there have been times when it paid off in tremendous ways." Jake turned as someone yelled his name. "Looks like I need to help David. I'll chat with you later."

"Okay, Jake." As he ran off, she wondered what tomorrow would hold. Olivia looked out at the ocean. Gray clouds were brewing over the water. She had no wish to be on the beach in a storm. After all, this area was one of the highest in lightning strikes.

Chapter Two

Olivia stood at the edge of her balcony, watching water fall in droplets all around her. Thunder woke her in the middle of the night but she let the sound of the rain lull her back to sleep.

Olivia texted Jake.

Are we going treasure hunting today since the weather is stormy?

Yep. Dress in layers and bring a raincoat if you have one.

Against her better judgment, Olivia got into the van and waited for the rest of the group to come. Only three more people decided to go. David sat behind the wheel. *What had happened to Jake?*

No one talked. They must be worried too. She should have dressed warmer, instead she had on a sundress with a light scarf. She'd brought a raincoat but didn't want to carry it around. It was warm even in the midst of the drizzle.

After unloading their equipment, Jake still had not shown. She took her metal detector and commenced scanning while she zig-zagged down the beach.

Time became irrelevant as her mind wandered. *What would it be like diving in the ocean? If we find the lost ship and its artifacts, will we be on the news?* A big discovery could turn into extra money for everyone along with the notoriety. Renting an apartment in Denver cost a lot. Maybe she could find a house to call home.

A sudden clap of thunder reverberated through the atmosphere and brought her back to the real world. She glanced around and didn't see anyone familiar. She turned to walk toward the area where the van should be. The drizzling rain began falling faster, and the droplets got bigger, pelting her in the face as the wind howled. Another loud crash echoed like a sonic boom as it erupted from the sky. Thick bolts of lightning burst from the heavens as the dark clouds brewed to the horizon. Her heart pounded as she pondered what to do.

No houses or hotels to be seen along this stretch of beach. If she dashed through the dense grass and palmettos covering the dunes, she might make it to a street. If not, she made the perfect lightning rod standing alone in the sand with a metal detector in her hand. Out of nowhere, another spike of light accompanied with eardrum shattering thunder struck the beach a hundred yards from her. The hair on her arms stood from the static electricity in the air. Olivia panicked, dropped the metal detector, and rushed into the towering grass on the dunes bordering the beach.

Too afraid to move, she laid in the grass berm shaking. Her thoughts shifted to snakes that might be hiding, which gave her the motivation to get up. She pushed up to her hands and knees and crawled through the grass. She had to keep hiking up her dress so she didn't rip it as she crawled.

Faster.

Faster.

Until the fear coursing through her body forced her to her feet.

She ran.

She had to get back to the group. *What if they leave without me?* Another outburst of thunder followed by a large lightning bolt hit near her, causing her to stumble and fall. She jumped up and returned to running. A tall man in an vintage suit appeared a few yards in front of her. Suddenly, the ground beneath her opened. Olivia screamed as everything went black. The hole turned in slow motion as she fell.

Oomph! Olivia landed on her stomach, the air knocked out of her lungs. She gasped for breath but didn't get any. She worried she might pass out. Finally, she drew in deep breaths and pushed herself up from the sand. She brushed her face off and opened her eyes. Her nerves grew tight. Darkness had settled.

What had happened? One minute she'd been running through the grass, the next falling through a hole only to face plant in the sand. The amount of time she fell made her fear the landing. It should've been much worse. The sound of ocean waves reassured her as she came down on the sand. *Was it the same beach*? How had it changed from day to night?

Did I lose consciousness? If I landed on the same beach and had been knocked out, wouldn't someone have noticed I went missing? Why hadn't Jake been there today? Jake would have made sure I was okay. She understood Florida was known for sinkholes, but most people didn't survive those. Could a sinkhole swallow a person and deposit them at a different time of day, or in a different place? It didn't make sense, and now she knelt alone in the darkness. A moment of panic hit her. She couldn't see a thing except for the full moon and its light reflecting off the ocean surf.

She stretched out each leg before standing. Everything seemed fine. Rain fell in a heavy drizzle, but she hadn't heard any thunder. She let out a sigh of relief and walked toward what she believed to be the way she had come. Although, at this point, confusion made it hard to think. *Why is it so dark?* She didn't see any lights on. *Is the power out from the storm?*

Her dress was soaked and the scarf missing. The thought of a hot bath in her hotel room never sounded so amazing. After that, she'd order room service and relax in her bed with a good book. Hearing a noise in the distance, she hastened her pace, hoping someone might help, but the darkness made her uneasy.

Walking down the coast, she spotted a glowing light in the distance. She heard voices and saw people near what she could now see was a fire. Sneaking closer, she could tell they were arguing. Worried. She moved into the grass. She crouched, then crawled closer to check out what was going on without them discovering her.

Olivia narrowed the distance and noticed a large group of men dressed in old-time military uniforms and ship lackeys from long ago. Were they having a cosplay party? She found that hard to believe, especially amid the rain.

They weren't speaking English, but a form of Spanish. Yes, definitely Catalan. She'd taken Spanish in high school and advanced courses in college. Her love of history led her to become a history professor. As she knelt in the grass, listening intently, she overheard them saying they needed to find water. *Isn't there a store nearby?*

Should she stay hidden or introduce herself? Maybe they could tell her which way to her hotel. She pulled out her cell phone, but it didn't turn on; nothing. Something must have happened to it when she fell. The wind had picked up, causing her to shiver. The fire looked so welcoming. Hopefully, they weren't criminals. Why hadn't she just stayed in her room this morning? She walked out of the grass and into the camp.

"Aturar! *Stop!*" One of the men pulled a sword from his scabbard.

Olivia froze. "Els i signifiquen cap mal. *I mean you no harm.*" *What is this guy doing? He took this costume party a little too literal.*

"I'm lost."

The man strode toward her. "Drop to your knees!" He motioned another guy over to her.

The other man pushed Olivia to her knees. Her hands shook. She had to remain in control and suppress the fear gripping her. *What have I wandered into?*

"How did you get here? Where did you come from?" The guy with the sword asked.

Another man shouted. "Look at her clothing. I've never seen a grown woman dress like in that manner."

"Are you a survivor from one of the other ships? None of the three women from our ship made it."

Oliva trembled. "I don't understand. What ships? Please don't hurt me!"

A third man walked in from the blackness. "What ships? The ships in our fleet. How could you not know? Our boat sunk off the coast during a horrific storm two weeks ago." He pointed toward the ocean waves crashing on the beach.

This man exuded an air of authority. She noticed the men step aside as he moved closer.

"I haven't heard about your ships. I'm on vacation and got lost. Olivia's voice cracked. I want to find the way back to my hotel."

The guy leaned in close to Olivia's face. "What is vacation and hotel? I don't understand these words." His breath made Olivia wince.

"I am Captain Gabriel Matias Rodriquez of the *Santismia Trinidad*. Who are you? How do you understand our language, but you are fair-skinned? You are wearing unusual clothes, Senyora. Where did you come from?

"My name is Olivia Hanson. I've had classes in Catalan. Sir. You should understand one's skin doesn't have to be a specific color in order to speak a language. I had not prepared for being on the beach tonight." Olivia stared into his eyes. "I fell through a hole in the sand today, and now I'm here."

He stared at her, wanting to determine if she told the truth. "Speak words I know." He said sternly. "You make no sense. No woman would dress in this manner unless she's not a dama, *lady*. You're wearing clothing we have never seen, and you describe things we've never heard of. No one falls through a hole in the beach. Are you loco?" Captain Rodriquez looked at the men, and they roared.

"I'm not mad." Tears streaked down her cheeks. "This doesn't make any sense. I need to get back to my room, eat and go to sleep. I don't recognize where I am or who you are, and I don't care about your ships. I never heard about any of this. Please don't harm me, I'm not a threat to you." Olivia put her hands over her face and sobbed.

Captain Rodriquez turned to his men. *"¿Puede estar diciendo la verdad" Can she be speaking the truth?"*

"Absolutely not, Captain. We can't trust her, she's not one of us. You must not fall for her tears, she may be a witch, sent to put a curse on everyone here."

Olivia lifted her head to see who spoke. It was the man who ordered her to fall to her knees.

"Antonio! I'm in charge here! This woman can not harm us. She is nothing. A lost soul. Bring her some water and food. Find a place for her to sleep tonight where she'll be safe. If anything happens to her, I'll hold you responsible and it won't go well for you. We'll consider what to do with her tomorrow." Captain Rodriquez walked back into the darkness.

Olivia cringed as Antonio untied her hands and yanked her to her feet. "You do not fool me, woman. I'll be watching you." He jerked her toward the fire. "Sit here." Antonio took a pot off the fire, scooped out something into a bowl. He handed it to her along with a cup of water.

She ate the mush with her fingers. She barely swallowed it without puking. It tasted like mold. Olivia wanted more water but didn't dare ask for any. When she stopped eating, Antonio brought her a ragged blanket and told her to lie down next to the fire. At least the beach sand made a nice cushion as she sunk into it. She covered herself with the blanket.

If the way the men stared at her was a sign of her vulnerability, then she better sleep with one eye open. Captain Rodriguez's threat kept her safe. She had many questions, but no answers. She had become a stranger in an unfamiliar land. None of this made any sense.

She feared for her life and had no idea how to get home. She wished to wake up from this bad dream. Her eyes grew heavy as the fire warmed her body. If nothing else, she appreciated the heat. Not even the bugs and the glaring stares of the surrounding men kept her awake.

Chapter Three

Rambunctious hollering startled Captain Gabriel Rodriguez from his sleep. He got up and walked to the opening of his shelter. He could see his men gathered in a group, laughing and telling jokes. He hadn't heard laughter from them since the night the storm shipwrecked them off the coast. They were lucky to be alive, as most of them hadn't survived. They'd lost friends and family. It had been a time of considerable grief.

They had been part of an eleven-ship fleet returning to Spain from Havana, Cuba. Gabriel had been told men from the other boats had survived as a few had made it up the coast to them. He hoped other ships showed up soon. The storm occurred over two weeks ago and they needed more provisions. Unless they were found by other Spaniards, it would most likely be pirates out to kill and rob them of the little treasure they'd been able to recover.

If pirates didn't, then the native tribes might try. There had been two skirmishes with the tribes who lived in the area of the shipwrecks. Three of his men had lost their lives hunting for food. His crewmen had the advantage in weapon strength over the natives clubs and knives. Unfortunately, they had not been able to save a lot of gun powder from their ship. The pirates, however, were equally armed. Gabriel had lost his sword in the storm as he'd left it in his cabin. He'd found another one on the beach, but it was not the same.

Yesterday, he sent ten of his crewmen for help on a long trek north to the Spanish settlement at St. Augustine. This morning, a few men left on a longboat hoping to follow the currents back to Cuba to get help.

Gabriel concentrated on hearing why his crewmen were laughing. It was then he remembered the woman who had stumbled into their camp last night. He left his shelter and walked over to the group. He saw her struggling to get up while one of the men tugging at the bottom of her dress.

"Didn't I say, to protect this woman, not harm her?" he roared.

"No one hurt her, just a little fun," Antonio explained.

"Let her go!"

The man holding the hem of her dress released it. She tumbled over onto her side.

Olivia glanced at Gabriel. "Thank you. Am I allowed to go to the bathroom?" She said as she got up and walked toward him.

Captain Rodriquez raked his fingers through his hair. He'd forgotten his hat. "The bathroom? I don't understand."

"I need to relieve myself, or nature is calling. I have to do what every human does multiple times a day. Do you know what I mean?"

Gabriel saw her cheeks turn a bright shade of pink. "You mean the 'head'? Squat up there in the tall grass and do what you need to." He laughed while pointing at the sand dunes. "Don't venture out of my sight. There are Indians around here. I'll give you a few minutes before I yell to make sure you're safe."

Gabriel walked back to his shelter. He had enough to be worried over without a woman being added to his list of responsibilities? He grabbed his hat off the ground where he'd fallen asleep and crammed it on his head. It didn't take long until the heat of the day made wearing it unbearable.

They'd never encountered a storm as bad as the one they barely made it through. It engulfed the sky and sent winds more fierce than any he'd ever experienced, running their ship aground, tearing it apart with ease. At the time, he wondered if they'd all perish.

Since then, a deceased body of one of their crewmen washed ashore every day. The crew had been recovering as much of the treasure and supplies that they could from what was left of their ship.

"Excuse me."

The woman startled him as she peeked into his shelter.

"You think I am some sort of spy or stowaway, but that is not true." Olivia walked into the shelter.

"Senyora, there is much about you I do not understand. How does a woman, dressed in her undergarments, wander into our camp unharmed? You had no way to protect yourself and then you speak of things I have no knowledge of, using words I've never heard. You look British, with your light skin, brown eyes, and blonde hair, but do not speak with a British accent. Other than the natives and the men who survived, there are no British settlements in this area. How can you explain this to me?"

"If I tell you the truth, you won't believe it. If I make up a lie, you won't believe it." Olivia looked away. "Can I ask you what year this is?"

"How can you not know the year? And you wonder why we think you're loco. It is seventeen hundred and fifteen, and it's the 17th day of August. Time has slowed since we landed on this God-forsaken shore."

Olivia leaned toward Gabriel, whispering. "This is what happened, although you'll accuse me of being a witch after I tell you. I swear that everything I say is the truth, yet I do not understand how it could be possible. I'm from the year 2015, three hundred years in the future. I was with a group of people on this very day, August 17th, who were searching for the very treasure you have lost.

I didn't realize how far I had wandered until it became stormy. Lightning was striking close, and I panicked. I ran through the tall grass along the sand dunes. Olivia pointed toward a space up the shore from them. "The ground gave way beneath me and I fell through a dark hole. I'm not sure how long as time slowed, but I landed on my stomach in the sand.

I walked down the shore and saw your campfire in the distance. As I got closer, I wondered if you and your men were part of a costume party and I hoped you'd help me find my hotel. A hotel is a building with multiple rooms, where people can live when away from home. My clothes are not considered undergarments in the year 2015. It's called a sundress and is appropriate for women to wear on the beach in the middle of summer." She took in a deep breath.

Gabriel looked into her eyes and they were unflinching. If she was lying, he couldn't tell. "You are telling me you're from the year 2015. You fell through a hole in the earth and traveled back in time three hundred years? Take me to the place where you landed." Gabriel motioned for her to go before him and they headed up the beach in the direction she had pointed.

They were about a half-mile away from camp when she paused and picked up a piece of jewelry from the sand. "This is one of my earrings, I must have lost it when I landed."

He looked at her ears. There was a single matching earring in her left ear. "If you fell into a hole, you would land at the bottom, not on the same beach three hundred years earlier."

"I can't explain it. It doesn't make sense. I want to go home, back to my time." Tears seeped from Olivia's eyes. "I keep wishing I'll wake up from this awful dream." Olivia sat in the sand. She covered her face with her hands and sobbed.

"I am sorry, Senyora, for whatever has caused you to come to this place and time. I find it hard to believe you traveled through time, but I see you think so and it is causing you considerable distress. I'm not sure how to help you. Let's walk along the grass and find this hole." Captain Rodriquez gathered shells, and arranged them in a stack, marking where she had found her earring. Gabriel extended his hand toward her.

Olivia wiped the tears from her cheeks and hesitantly took his hand.

"Senyora, I can assure you I'm no monster, nor do I have any ulterior motives. You are safe with me, however, I can't say the same thing about many of the men. Be on guard at all hours." The touch of her hand in his stirred emotions he'd not felt in a long time. He shoved them away, releasing her hand after he pulled her to her feet.

"Let's walk around the beach."

They wandered around looking in the grass, grabbing anything unusual, but there was no sign of a hole in the ground. He walked toward the ocean and stared at the vast expanse of water. Olivia stood beside him. The wind was picking up and ominous dark clouds were heading their way. "We should go back to camp. Another storm is rolling in. We've built some small shelters just inland off the beach. They're not much, but it's better than being out in the open."

Thunder rattled in the distance. He watched her shudder as she glanced at the sky. He realized she'd been through something terrible, but was uncertain of what it could be. As a leader of men, he'd become adept at reading people's faces, and had a good record of ascertaining when individuals were lying. Maybe she'd experienced something so dreadful that her mind made this up to protect her. But that didn't explain how she got here.

Gabriel glanced at her as they walked back. She looked fragile. He felt a tug in his heart, as if, God was telling him to protect her. He wondered what that might cost him. She was a lost soul, possibly in a lost time. He needed to find her suitable clothing, even if it meant wearing a man's uniform. That just may be a good idea. He realized she was an enticement to his crewmen. They'd consider it a challenge to be the first to have their way with her, no matter how much he threatened them.

There was only one thing he could do, and the sooner the better.

Chapter Four

Olivia stared in disbelief at Captain Rodriquez. What had he said? Did he just tell her they needed to be married? Why? How? She couldn't marry him. When they examined the spot she'd found her lost earring at, she kept hoping a hole would open again and she'd drop back into the year twenty-fifteen. Olivia had read books and watched movies where the main character traveled to a different time, but those were fantasy novels, not reality, right? Had someone slipped drugs into her food at the hotel and she was hallucinating?

Captain Rodriquez offered her water from his leather flask as they took a brief break. The cool liquid brought relief to her parched throat. An older man walked toward them from the camp.

He smiled at her. "You must be Olivia. My name is Louis. The captain told me you wandered into camp at dusk. I kept watch last night so didn't hear the ruckus. He said you're uncertain of how you ended up here. Were you injured and perhaps lost your memory? Or captured and left here by pirates? Were you a passenger on one of the other ships?"

Olivia looked at Louis, unable to form answers to

his questions. Her mind wasn't processing anything beyond marrying Captain Rodriquez.

"I have just told Olivia she needs to marry me and I'm afraid she's speechless. It's the only answer for keeping her from being the focus of every man's thoughts. Some men will no longer entertain the idea of her being available out of respect for me, some will do it out of fear of what punishment they would receive and some won't care. Otherwise, these men won't stop until they are the first, to uh…, how do I convey this… take your virtue. Unfortunately, they have plenty of time to get into trouble as there is not enough to keep them busy. Rescue may be awhile, yet." Gabriel looked out to sea.

Louis put his hand on her shoulder. "I'm sure you never expected to hear those words. It must be quite a shock. The captain worries for your safety and wants to protect you. I'll have to think and pray on this, but you are probably right, Gabriel. These men have no honor. I've been with Captain Rodriquez since he was a small boy. He will protect you and stand by his word. He's thinking of your safety. Gabriel is a God-fearing man."

Louis had kind eyes peeking from beneath the wrinkles of his sun and sea weathered skin. She wondered why the captain cared. He accused her of being loco. From what Olivia had studied in history, the Captains of these ships were barely above the actions of their crewmen. *I can't marry a stranger.* Her stomach twisted in knots as she realized she had no say in the matter. She didn't have the freedoms to which she was accustomed to.

Before she came here, she'd often thought about how little she had, but now she understood the true meaning of the phrase. She only had the clothes on her back. The hopelessness of the circumstances she found herself in seeped into her soul. She had nowhere to go. If she escaped, there was only forest and swamps. She had no wilderness survival skills and would probably be raped and killed by the violent tribes or pirates in this part of Florida. Captain Rodriquez and Louis might be the only men who survived these shipwrecks who had a shred of decency.

"I never imagined the first time I asked a woman to marry me, she would take so long to say yes." The sides of the captain's mouth curved upwards.

Olivia understood he was trying to calm her nerves. Marrying him was her only option, but she couldn't meet his eyes as she realized what he'd expect of her. She'd only kissed a couple of men. She hadn't allowed it to go farther, not because of any religious or moral convictions, but because her life had been too busy. First with school and studying, then with her career as a history professor along with her other responsibilities. Then there was the slight problem she had with commitment well, actually, it would be the big problem.

The captain touched her hand.

She jumped.

"You have no alternative, Senyora. While you are in my care, I will do everything necessary to protect you. I won't expect you to do anything you aren't ready for. This marriage is in name only for as long as you want it to be. Although, I'd ask you to listen and do what I say because you can't survive alone. You will live with me in my shelter. Our marriage has to be regarded by others as a binding commitment.

If an opportunity happens for you to return to where you're from, you'll be free to go. Louis was a priest and can perform our ceremony and it will be legal. We should have a formal ceremony in the presence of the crewmen. They need to believe we are husband and wife in every sense. Only Louis and the two of us will know differently."

Gabriel looked at Louis. "See if you can find any women's clothing among the trunks and something for her hair."

Did he read my thoughts? Olivia followed him back to camp. He'd soon be her husband, and she'd be lying if that did not intrigue her. However, those feelings quickly disappeared as fear gripped her stomach, making it tough to breathe.

~

Olivia stood beside the captain. He held her hand and looked straight ahead at Louis. She was pledging her life to this man. Although, he had to nudge her with his elbow when it was her time to repeat her vows. Her thoughts were flying everywhere.

"I now pronounce you husband and wife." Louis proclaimed.

"Captain Gabriel Matias Rodriquez you may kiss your bride." Louis smiled as Captain Rodriquez turned toward her for the first time since the wedding ceremony began. Louis had found a veil amongst the few pieces of women's clothing they were able to salvage from the trunks.

A man as handsome as Gabriel would have women vying for his attention wherever he went. His long curly black hair was held back in a ponytail, and his tanned chiseled face made him the classic pirate movie lead actor. If she drew him for a poster, he'd resemble Johnny Depp in *Pirates of the Caribbean.*

As Gabriel lifted her veil, the warmth from his fingers touching her cheek sent expectations of things to come. He tenderly raised her chin with his hand as his lips claimed hers. It was no chaste kiss. Feelings unlike any she had ever experienced shot through her body. Her hands rested on his chest. Someone coughed, and she stumbled back, ending their kiss. She looked into his dark brown eyes and saw something more than kindness.

They stood there, as if frozen, staring at each other. She didn't understand what had just happened between them, they were strangers. It was more than she had expected.

Louis cleared his throat and broke the spell between them. "I now present to every man here on this beach, and in the sight of God, Captain Gabriel Matias Rodriquez, third son of King Philip V of Spain, and his wife Princess Olivia Suzanne Hanson Rodriquez. Those whom God has brought together may no one do anything to separate."

Olivia must have heard wrong. Her husband was a son to the king of Spain. This was all too much. She glanced at Captain Rodriquez, but he stared straight ahead again.

"We'd normally have a celebration, but because of our present circumstances, we'll postpone the grand affair. Instead, the evening will be spent eating dried beef and whatever else we can find." Louis dismissed the men to get back to what they needed to do for the night.

She looked out to sea. The sun was setting over the ocean and the golds and oranges were deeper tonight than they'd been since she arrived in Florida. A midday storm had blown over with a few wind gusts and showers of rain.

Captain Rodriquez took her hand and led her toward his shelter. He'd been working on it during the afternoon while she had been looking for clothes. He'd built a door and straightened the structure so it didn't lean so much.

"Olivia, this marriage won't be easy. It has to look legitimate to the men to keep you safe. If something were to happen to me, stay close to Louis and make sure you have weapons you can defend yourself with. I trust no one beyond him. I presume you've never had to protect yourself, so I'll teach you how to use a dagger." Captain Rodriquez opened the new door. He picked her up and carried her inside.

It was over so fast she didn't have time to object. There were a few blankets spread out to make a bed, a couple of wooden trunks being used for chairs, a makeshift table and lantern, and a few other odds and ends.

"Welcome home, Mrs. Rodriquez."

Olivia couldn't decide where to stand. She moved over to the table. "I understand why you thought I should marry you, but I don't think we'll convince them this is anything but what it is: a farce. They will certainly see through this. Why didn't you mention your father is the king of Spain?"

"It didn't matter. We have plenty of other matters to deal with." Gabriel went over and lit the lamp. "Would it have made a difference? There was no alternative."

Someone tapped on the door.

"Come in." Captain Rodriquez turned as Louis walked in with two bowls. "Here is your supper."

"Thank you, Louis. I want to teach Mrs. Rodriquez

how to defend herself. I'll need your help with this. Would you mind working with her tomorrow morning?" Captain Rodriquez moved to the center of the room where embers smoldered inside a rock circle. A hole in the roof allowed the smoke to escape. He stirred the coals and soon a small flame sprung to life. He put pieces of dead tree branches he had picked up in the woods on the flames.

"I'll help however I can."

"Thank you, Louis."

Louis left as Captain Rodriquez built the fire up. Soon the small space became warm, a little too warm.

"We'll be sleeping together. It's not unusual for the men to come in here unannounced when I'm needed. They must assume we have a real marriage. Louis found a second dress in the trunks that floated ashore. That will give you two to change out. You can wear your things at night. I'd only sleep in them. It wouldn't be appropriate to wear them around the other men." Gabriel took off his jacket. "I'll turn my back to you while you change your clothes and get in bed.

Olivia's hands shook as she unbuttoned her gown as far as she was able. However, it was not enough to enable her to take it off. She didn't want to ask for help. Louis had helped her put it on before the wedding, which had made her extremely uncomfortable. Now she needed help to get out of it, and her new husband was the logical choice. "I need assistance to get in or out of this dress. I've never worn anything like this before, but one person can't do this by themselves."

"Spin around. I am not a lady's maid, but I will try my best."

Every time the captain's fingers brushed her skin as

he unfastened buttons and untied laces it caused her nerves to be on edge. Partially from fear, but also from the feelings it brought to life. When he'd finally finished, she breathed a sigh of relief. Having to go through this twice a day was unimaginable.

"You can do the rest now, Olivia. I'm turning back around."

Olivia stepped out of the dress, slipped on her sundress, and burrowed under the blankets in record time. How did women wear those heavy gowns every day? It must weigh fifty pounds. "I'm done."

Captain Rodriquez took his shirt off.

She took a quick peek before she turned over. All was as expected, muscular and fit. She laid on her side with her back to him and attempted to relax. Uneasiness crept around inside of her as she wondered if he was a man of his word. Her heart raced as he pulled the blankets back and got under them? Their legs touched, and he quickly scooted over.

"Would you agree to do something with me each night before we fall asleep?"

Olivia turned over to see him staring up at the sky through the hole in their shelter. "What?"

"I would like to pray with you. For our safety."

"Pray? You are religious?"

Captain Rodriquez looked at her. "I believe in God, yes. And in his son, Jesus. I try to live my life the way He would want me to. I don't always succeed, but it's important to me."

"If you want to. I don't see a reason to, but if it makes you feel better than I will." Olivia could no longer keep eye contact with him. This was so weird.

As Gabriel prayed, she imagined God sitting in the

room with them. He was having a conversation with Him instead of speaking words to an imaginary being. Olivia relaxed the more he prayed. Her eyes closed, and she drifted off to sleep.

Chapter Five

Gabriel opened his eyes. A woman's arm hugged his chest and her head laid on his shoulder. Silky blonde hair fanned out in waves behind her. This woman was beautiful. Her long lashes rested on pink rosy cheeks. When they'd kissed yesterday, he hadn't expected such a strong reaction. What had he got himself into?

Her breathing was slow and gentle, still in a peaceful slumber. He hoped he'd be able to keep her safe in these circumstances. She didn't understand how this marriage had changed his life.

He was betrothed to the King of France's daughter to establish a stronger alliance between their two countries. His family and her family would not be pleased. They'd be furious. Wars had been fought over such breaches in a contract. He wondered if it might be better to live in this new territory, then face the wrath of his decision to marry Olivia. No one would understand his reasons.

His father might demand he annul his marriage or he'll disinherit him. Gabriel had made a vow before God to take care of Olivia, and he planned to honor it.

Whether he loved her or not, he would be the best husband possible to her.

The door opened. "Captain Rodriquez, there is a ship on the horizon."

"Friend or Foe?"

"Too far away to tell, but I assumed you would want to know."

"Thank you, Antonio. I'll be out shortly and next time knock."

He watched Antonio gaze upon Olivia. The man's eyes narrowed. He was becoming more brazen with his disdain and lack of respect. Gabriel had to remember he had enemies.

"Yes, captain," Antonio replied as he hurried out.

~

Olivia woke up. "I'm so sorry. I didn't know I was lying on you. How embarrassing."

"I didn't mind. We better get dressed. There is a ship sighted off the coast. I pray it's here to help and not to loot. Stay in the shelter until I come for you. If it's pirates, then hide until they leave. I'll have Louis take you somewhere safe. I'll also have him tie your gown." Gabriel got up, put his clothes on, and went to check on the ship. The absence of his body next to hers left Olivia chilled. She was able to put her dress on but was grateful when Louis came to help with the buttons and ribbons.

Louis pulled the laces tight and tied them.

Olivia wished she had her comfy jeans and a t-shirt. "One would expect these dresses to be constructed in a way where it didn't take two people to get dressed."

"The type of women who wear these dresses have

maids to serve them. When we get to Spain, as the wife of the King's son, you will have plenty of help." Louis laughed. "I can't say I ever thought I would fill in as a lady's maid." He patiently waited while she brushed her hair and braided it.

"I'm not sure I want to go to Spain," Olivia said

"Olivia, you're not thinking clearly. How would you take care of yourself here? This marriage was not only for your safety here but for your protection when we get back to Spain. You have nothing here or there. You are now married to the King's son, and he's third in line to the throne. It would be in your best interest to go with your husband. You have been blessed with an opportunity no one would've imagined. If I can be so bold, it would behoove you to provide successors."

Olivia choked.

"I'm sorry I had to be so blunt. Gabriel's family won't make it easy for the two of you, but a baby would encourage the King and Queen to accept this marriage. You will be properly taken care of as the mother of his children."

"I can't leave here or I will never be able to go home." Olivia's voice broke.

"Where is home?" Louis asked. "When I first met you, you gave me no answers."

"I'm not sure anymore. My parents are deceased. I have no other family, and I am alone." Olivia's eyes teared up.

"Why would you care then if you traveled to Spain? There is nobody for you here. However, you are never alone, Senyora. There is One who always loves you." Louis looked toward the door. "Maybe marrying Captain Rodriquez is God's answer to your loneliness."

"God has never been with me. Nothing has happened when I've prayed."

"I'm sorry you are hurting, Olivia. Many times God intervenes and we are not aware of it. He always answers our prayers, however, we may not like the answer. I will be praying for you. God loves you. I should get us some water."

So much had taken place that Olivia's head was reeling. Her stomach was nauseous. She needed to leave the shelter and look for a way to get back to her time. She peeked out the door, no one was near, so she left.

She snuck through the tall grass until she got far enough away no one could see her. She found the circle of rocks they had made yesterday where her earring had been found. She walked along the beach, back and forth, trying to cover every inch of sand. She ventured closer to the dunes.

Her stomach growled and her mouth was dry. She should head back, Sweat ran down her body under the cumbersome gown. She longed for her sundress. If she got her legs wet in the ocean, it might cool her off. She went to the water's edge and let the waves splash over her feet, time after time. She almost forgot her troubles. She remembered doing this a few days ago at the beach. Why did it seem like years, not days?

How had a hole opened up and transferred her to the same place three hundred years earlier? If she came through it, there had to be a way for her to go back. What was she missing?

Suddenly, a shrieking yell pierced her ears. Before she could move, a hand slapped over her face and covered her mouth. She struggled to scream as she was being dragged backward. She went limp, which allowed her to slide out of her captor's arms. She got up to run but stumbled as her foot caught in the hem of the heavy gown she was wearing.

She saw the painted face of her attacker out of the corner of her eye as he snatched a handful of her hair and yanked her backward. Excruciating pain shot through her head as she screamed and kicked, but he only pulled harder. He paused at the edge of the grass and punched her in the stomach, knocking the air from her lungs. Her body convulsed as she sought to regain her breath. He stared into her eyes. Indians. She should have listened to Louis. He gripped her arm and jerked her toward him. He put a knife to her throat. Fear overcame her, causing her to shake uncontrollably. His eyes were dark and lifeless.

To her left, there were three more Indian men. He yelled at her in his language and shook her as if she was refusing to answer.

"Let me go," Olivia screamed.

He shoved her backward onto the sand, said something to the other men. She presumed they were deciding her fate, and it didn't look encouraging. He knelt next to her, breathing heavily into her face. He grabbed her hair, yanking her head back as he ground his mouth into hers. Olivia tried to spit and scream but could not overcome the assault. He tugged at the front of her dress as she flailed. His open hand slapped her so hard, she saw a flash of light and realized she might die.

A sudden boom echoed. It pulled her back from slipping into unconsciousness.

The Indian crumpled to the ground beside her, bleeding profusely from his skull. His grasp on her hair loosened and she moved away as fast as her legs would work. The other braves ran as more shots rang out, causing one of them to slam face-first into the sand. She spun to see Captain Rodriquez running toward her.

"Olivia, are you hurt?"

Olivia stared at him. Her mind was numb and she couldn't remember how to talk.

Gabriel scooped her up in his arms. He took a step and suddenly they were falling.

Chapter Six

Olivia landed on the beach as before. No longer in the comfort and protection the captain's arms offered. The wind whirled around her and thunder cracked in the distance. What had happened? She rolled onto her back and took a deep breath. Everything had taken place so fast she had yet had a chance to calm her nerves. One minute she'd expected to die, the next safely scooped up into Gabriel's arms. *Where is Gabriel?* Olivia looked to her right. Nothing. Then to her left. She saw him about twenty feet away. He wasn't moving. She struggled to stand, but her legs were like jelly and her jaw hurt from being slapped. She crawled to him and shook his shoulders.

"Gabriel, are you okay?" Nothing. She checked for a pulse. It was there. Olivia tried pushing him onto his side. Blood trickled down his face as she lifted his head from the sand. There was a small rock under it. *He must've hit it when he landed.* She managed to get him turned over, and he started to moan.

A man in a security uniform yelled to them. "Hey lady, are you and the pirate all right? Must've been quite a party for you both to end up passed out on the beach in those costumes in the midst of a storm."

"We're fine, sir. I'm sorry, we'll be on our way soon."

Olivia smiled as she realized she was back to present day. She put her hand over the side of her face that was injured in case the officer came closer.

"Gabriel, can you move?" Olivia bent down to examine his wound.

"What happened, my head hurts?" He tried to sit up but collapsed. "The world is spinning."

"Stay still. You've hit your head on a rock and you're bleeding. We fell through the time portal and traveled to my time. I'm sorry you came through with me. I don't understand why this is happening."

Olivia breathed a sigh of relief as there weren't many people around. She didn't recognize where she was, but presumed they were on the same beach in Florida where she stayed. Hopefully, they were near her hotel. She needed to get Gabriel there and then buy clothes for him.

Gabriel sat up. "Your time period? That's impossible. This can't be real. I suspected you'd been abused by captors and lost your memory and imagined you were from the future."

Olivia stood and reached for the captain's hand. "The sooner you can get to your feet, the better. We have to find my hotel so you can change into some present-day clothing." She helped him up. "I don't have any money or a phone?"

Gabriel wobbled as he stood up. "Olivia, you must've hit your head too what you're saying makes no sense."

Olivia pointed down the shore to where multi-story hotels stood. "Look around. Tell me you are in 1715."

Captain Rodriquez looked both ways. His face no longer had the same composed expression on it. "Did you do something to me?"

"No, don't you remember. You rescued me from the man who attacked me, picked me up, and took a step, then we fell through the sand. The same way it happened to me before. There isn't an explanation, but now we are in 2015.

I wonder what day it is. Hopefully, I still have my room. I came here to search for treasure from your ships. If we are near, we won't have to go far. Can you walk?" Olivia gripped his elbow.

"I'm fine now. I must go back to my time, my brother, and Spain. I can't walk to your room or whatever you call it." Captain Rodriquez wandered in circles around the area, but nothing happened.

"It must open only at specific times. There seems to be no reason why it does. We can check later, but for now, we have to buy you some clothes" Olivia started walking in the direction she remembered her hotel was. She glanced back. He hadn't moved. She continued toward the hotels. He caught up to her.

"I can't stay here wherever this is."

"We're on the same Florida coast where your ships ran aground, except in the year 2015. We are three hundred years in the future. It must be overwhelming to you. It was to me to find myself in your time." Olivia smiled, trying to calm him as they trudged along the beach.

Gabriel looked out to sea. "Who is doing this and why? It couldn't have occurred without someone making it, at least I don't think so. I can't even believe I am saying it is possible."

"It is all too crazy to be real, but yet it is. We are living it." Olivia pointed down the beach. "There's my hotel. Follow me and let me do the talking."

Gabriel looked around in astonishment at this unfamiliar world. "I can't even hope to understand all of this."

They walked through the rear entrance into the hotel and made their way to the front desk. The clerk's eyes widened as he saw their clothes. "Can I help you?"

"Yes, sir. My name is Olivia Hanson, and I have misplaced my room key card."

The desk clerk ignored the ringing phone. "What's your room number?"

"354"

The young man typed on his computer. "Okay, Miss Hanson. Can I see your ID?

"I'm sorry, it's in my room."

"That's ok, what's your birthdate?"

Oliva gave him her birthdate. He pulled open a drawer behind him. "Here's your spare card. Hope you had a good time at the costume party, Miss Hanson." The clerk laughed.

"We did. Thank you, sir." She breathed a sigh of relief. She was surprised he didn't ask about Gabriel's cut and blood or her red cheek and eye. He must have thought it was part of their costume. She wondered if this was the night of the day she first fell through the hole, as she still had her reservation.

Olivia put her hand on Gabriel's elbow. "This way." She pressed the button on the elevator.

"What is this?" Captain Rodriquez looked ready to

run.

"It's a small room which takes you to different floors or levels, instead of using stairs." Olivia stepped into the elevator and motioned Gabriel in. He walked inside, but she realized he had to be unsure. She pushed the third-floor button. When the elevator began moving, Gabriel threw his arms out and braced himself against the wall.

The doors opened, and he followed her to her room. She used the key to open the door and was happy to see everything was as she had left it. She had stored her purse in the safe. It would've been too heavy to carry it and the metal detector. All her meals were included in the trip, so she hadn't needed any money.

"Let me clean that cut." She grabbed a cloth and cleaned it off. "I'm going to change into different clothes." Olivia asked Gabriel to undo all the ties on her gown, hopefully for the last time. She grabbed a skirt and blouse and took off the heavy dress. She hadn't picked the shorts and tank top as she didn't want Gabriel to pass out from the indecency of her clothing. She could only imagine what he would think of them. When she came out of the bathroom, he was very quiet. "Are you all right?"

"I'm confused, and it seems I'm in a dream. It's impossible to travel through time, yet here we are." He ran his hand through his black hair. There are poles that light up without candles or torches. Doors and small rooms that move by themselves.

"I understand. I faced the same emotions you are. Let's take it a day at a time and see what we can figure out. I'll order food for tonight and then tomorrow I will call an Uber to take me to a store to purchase clothes for you. I'm sorry you don't understand what I just said. I'm asking someone to bring us food and get me to a place where I can buy clothing. Although, I have to guess what size you wear. I'll care for you in my world as you did with me in yours." Olivia picked up the hotel phone and dialed room service.

"I can take care of myself. I don't need a woman to do that." Gabriel stood and walked to the window.

"I know you can. But it will be easier once you figure out how things work, what acceptable behavior is, and what isn't. How to dress, and how to operate these fascinating objects you see all around you. Please trust me. Just as you advised me I should with you. It wouldn't be hard to get lost or have someone do something to you. I'll pick up two cell phones tomorrow for both of us and teach you how to use them. They are little boxes we can communicate to each other through, even if we're far away." Olivia put her hand on his arm. "I'm sorry for getting you caught up in this."

"Olivia, I'm not blaming you. We both have been pawns. We have to figure out what makes this transpire. It has something to do with being on the beach. It has happened when you've been frightened. First the storm and later the attack. I don't know why it brought me with you. Is some higher power creating the connection between time periods?" Gabriel stared into her eyes. "God must be upset with me."

"I doubt God truly cares about us at all if there even is a God. Why would He choose to drop me into the past? Who am I? This could be happening to other people. They aren't saying anything for fear of someone thinking they're crazy. You are right. Both times I passed through time, I was terrified."

A knock sounded on her door.

"It must be our food." Olivia opened the door.

The service boy wheeled in a food cart. Olivia tipped him as he left. She lifted the covers off the dishes. "I ordered something very popular. It's called a cheeseburger and french fries." She set the plates on the small table. "Let's eat."

They both sat.

Gabriel studied how she took a bite of the cheeseburger and did the same. Then he popped a few fries into his mouth.

"Do you like it?" she asked.

"It's unusual. Many flavors. I'd rather have a deer leg cooked over a fire, but I will eat it." Gabriel was hungry as he ate everything on his plate.

Olivia picked up the lid of another dish to expose two slices of chocolate cake with chocolate frosting and two large scoops of vanilla ice cream. "Gabriel, this is one of my favorite desserts."

"This is good." Gabriel smiled.

"It's the best." Olivia smiled back.

Gabriel leaned back in his chair.

"Oh, I should explain some things to you."

She took him to the bathroom and showed him how the toilet worked and the reasoning behind it. She demonstrated the sinks, shower, and bathtub. Gabriel was impressed. She told him to take a bath or shower while she ran across the street to Walmart to buy him pajamas.

~

She came back with underwear and pajamas, hoping

she'd guessed the right size.

When she opened the door, Gabriel was sitting in a chair with a towel wrapped around his waist. She was at a loss for words. She tried but failed to avert her eyes from him as she explained the clothing uses. He went to change. When he walked out, he looked like a different man. No more Spanish captain, but instead a handsome man on vacation in Florida.

"How do you like your pajamas?" Olivia asked.

"They are very soft."

"I'm going to put my pajamas on and then we can get some sleep."

"Pajamas?"

"Clothes that are made for sleeping in."

Olivia changed in the bathroom, then climbed into bed. "I assume since we were married three hundred years ago, it's still fine for you to sleep next to me. Besides, there isn't another bed in here."

Gabriel got into bed. "Forgive me for doubting what you told me. You spoke the truth even though it sounded absurd."

Olivia fluffed her pillow. "I don't blame you. It was inconceivable to me too until I experienced it."

"I can't continue in this time, Olivia. I see how happy you are to be back, but this is not how I live. My heart is so heavy tonight. You must've had the same emotions." Gabriel touched her cheek and looked deeply into her eyes. "You're beautiful, Olivia. You're cheek and eye look like they are going to bruise. Does it hurt? I have no suggestions on where we go from here, other than I have to find a way back."

"No," she answered. "Well, it stings."

He said I'm beautiful. Olivia wondered what was in

store for them. She didn't wish to live in his world, and he didn't want to continue in hers. She sensed a connection with him. Could he ever be happy here? It wasn't looking good so far. Time would tell. Olivia turned over. The events of the day had exhausted her, her eyes kept closing every few minutes, and it didn't take long before she fell into a peaceful sleep.

Chapter Seven

Gabriel opened his eyes. The reality of where he was hit him hard. He'd married a woman from a different time. His chivalry in protecting her from his men and compassion for a perceived calamity he envisioned she'd suffered changed his life, possibly forever. She had been telling the truth, and now he might never get back. Not seeing his family again, or doing the things he loved, became bigger than he could handle. He couldn't fathom having to remain here.

He turned over and looked at Olivia sleeping next to him. Her body rose and fell in a gentle rhythm, and he assumed it was the first time she'd slept peacefully since falling into his time. Gabriel's compassion increased for what she'd gone through now that he had experienced how hopeless it was. He studied everything in the room. Life changed immensely in the past three hundred years. The enormity of it, he had only begun to realize.

He gently pushed a strand of her hair from her eyes. This woman understood so much more than he did. What if he never returned? How would he create a new life? He tried going back to sleep, but his mind swirled with unanswered questions. He wanted to search for the portal. Hopefully, they had missed something in their hurry to get off the beach before more people wondered what they were doing.

Olivia stirred, opening her eyes.

Gabriel sat up. "I turned over to see if you were awake but ended up watching you sleep. You look so beautiful and peaceful when you are dreaming. I'd like to return to the beach to determine if we missed something."

Olivia agreed and got up to get ready. She ordered room service using the communication box again. He liked the breakfast food better than what he'd eaten last night.

Olivia left to get him clothes while he took a shower. He didn't understand why people washed so much. A waste of time and soap.

When she returned, they made their way to the location they'd fallen through, but there wasn't any sign that a hole had opened up. They were so absorbed in looking they didn't notice the treasure hunting team arrive.

Jake strode toward them. "Hi, Olivia. What happened to your cheek? It looks like you may have a black eye in a day or so. We tried to find you yesterday after the storm rolled in. I showed up late as I had an appointment. We searched for a bit, but you were nowhere to be seen. We assumed you ran back to the hotel on your own. I wondered why you weren't in the lobby this morning. I see you decided to come out on your own. Will your friend be joining us today?"

"Hi Jake, this is my good friend Gabriel. I fell down the stairs in the hotel. Thought I would get some exercise instead of using the elevator. My flip flop caught on the edge of a step. I'm sorry. The storm scared me a bit, and I did go back to my room. I tried to find everyone but didn't see you. I must've got turned around. I met Gabriel this morning for breakfast and he wanted to see what we do. I hope that's okay. He flew in from Colorado last night."

Jake extended his hand to Gabriel, and he shook it.

Olivia and Jake talked for a few minutes while Gabriel waited. He didn't recognize the meaning of many of the words they spoke. When they finished, Jake left.

"Gabriel, do you want to search the beach for coins from your ships?" Olivia's face lit up.

"I have nothing better to do? Of course, I need to search more."

Gabriel walked back toward the grass. Olivia got a long stick with a circle at the end.

"Okay, let's discover something of value from your ship." Olivia went to retrieve the metal detector.

"What does that do?" Gabriel kept in step with her.

"It can detect if there are items buried in the sand that contain metal, such as gold and silver. It makes a sound for us to hear if it locates something."

Right on cue, it beeped. Olivia dug in the sand and pulled out a quarter. "Definitely not treasure from your time. This is a coin from mine. It's called a 'quarter', and it won't buy much, but can be used with other coins and paper money to purchase things."

They continued searching for a few hours but didn't recover anything else. Olivia gave the metal detector back, and they left for the hotel.

Gabriel chose to stay in the hotel while Olivia went to buy what she called 'cell phones'. She said that they were communication boxes used to talk to each other when they weren't in the same place. He was overwhelmed with all the new things this world offered. He wondered if Louis and his men were searching for them. They probably assumed they'd been taken captive by the Indians. He struggled to put into words how he felt, he realized he wasn't made for this time. He was of no importance here. He needed to pray.

God, help me see why you allowed this to happen. I've sought to do what you'd have me do, be who you asked me to be, but this is too high of a cost. Why did you let me marry a woman who wasn't even born until three hundred years later? Am I to remain in this age? God, I don't want this. Please help me understand.

Gabriel eyes closed.

Chapter Eight

Olivia faced another day of uncertainty. Gabriel had been asleep when she came back from the store last night and he remained sleeping. He battled between anger and fear from being snatched from his time, which she recognized as she'd just went through it herself. If Olivia could find a way to get him back to 1715 and her stay here, it might be the best possible answer. It would be hard to let him go. She'd miss him. She had never met anyone even remotely like him.

Breakfast should be delivered any minute. She wanted to continue with the treasure hunting but didn't know if he would be up to it. She hadn't told Gabriel her flight back to Denver left in two days. Olivia didn't know how to bring it up. He wouldn't want to leave here, it might be his only chance to get home. Would the portal open without her, or had it opened for the last time? She couldn't leave him in Florida alone. Gabriel would have no means or knowledge to survive. Why had this happened to them? She wanted answers. She'd done the *Ancestry.com* thing before but hadn't delved very deep into it.

Gabriel coughed. Olivia checked his forehead. It

was hot.

Knock. Knock. Knock.

Olivia opened the door to let room service in with their breakfast. As soon as they left, she tried to get Gabriel out of bed, but he didn't move, he just groaned. She ate a few bites while watching him sleep. She decided to run to Walmart and buy Tylenol and a thermometer for him.

~

When she returned, Gabriel was gone. *Why would he leave, he's sick?*

She rushed to the lobby but didn't see him. Olivia ran out onto the beach and still no sign of him. He must have gone looking for the way back. She jogged up and down the coast to find him, but no luck. She struggled to breathe because fear pressed down on her chest and made her stomach cramp. *Where did he go?* Olivia ran back to the hotel, then up the stairs to their room. The elevator would've taken too long. He sat outside their door.

"Where have you been? I've been so worried!" Olivia touched the back of her hand to his forehead. "You are hot."

"When I woke up you had left, I looked for you downstairs and out on the beach. It didn't take me long to get lost, and I panicked." Gabriel leaned his head against the door. "I feel awful."

"I'm so glad you found your way back. I can't imagine how you felt. I assumed you'd sleep while I went to a store to get you some medicine. Please don't leave the room again without me." Olivia opened the door. Gabriel struggled to his feet, walked to the bed, and flopped down.

"I prayed." Gabriel pulled the blanket over him.

At this point, Olivia's head hurt too, so she showed him how to take Tylenol. She placed a cool washcloth on his forehead. He took the medicine and fell asleep. She breathed a sigh of relief and plopped into a chair. *Why would he leave the room?* She looked at the unopened cell phone boxes on the table. She needed to get them going. It would've helped in this instance.

While he dozed, she pulled out her laptop and researched her family history. She logged into her account on *Ancestry.com*. Using the service, she made connections on her father's side, taking her back to the mid-19th century. She found an article in a local British newspaper about a cousin.

The article described him as quite strange. His name was Gregory Hanson and his neighbors considered him to be something of a, 'mad scientist.' Mostly a recluse, he stayed home working on all kinds of inventions. One of them, in particular, involved time travel, and in the story, he boasted he traveled through time often. He ultimately died alone, without his claim ever proven.

Olivia didn't know if this helped or not. Finding him in her father's family seemed more than coincidental after what happened to her. Maybe he was the key to this mystery? Under ordinary circumstances, reading a story such as this would make her laugh. She'd have thought him crazy, but having gone through time twice, she couldn't argue it was possible.

Gabriel's voice pierced the dead air in the room. "Olivia, would you get me some water?"

She started as she'd forgotten he was there. "Of course. How are you doing?"

"Aaahh, not too great."

Olivia took him a cup of water and touched his forehead with her hand. Still hot. She took out the thermometer she'd bought from its package and checked his temperature. One hundred and two. She brought him a couple more pain relievers, and sat next to him, holding his hand. He quickly fell back asleep.

She wondered if any cafes made homemade chicken noodle soup. She checked online and found a local restaurant that delivered. If she needed to take him to a doctor or hospital, he had no identification, they might refuse to see him. This adventure she'd gotten herself into become more complex by the day. She used to complain her life lacked excitement. She now realized an uneventful life might be a gift.

Soon a tap on the door alerted her to the delivery driver. Olivia paid the man, then sat a plastic bag on the table. The delicious chicken aroma filled the room. The soup had arrived.

Olivia gently nudged Gabriel's shoulder. "Wake up, you need to eat."

He opened his eyes.

"I have some soup for you, Gabriel. It should help." Olivia handed him the Styrofoam bowl and buttered roll.

He sat up and slurped the soup. "Mmm, this is good."

"It's chicken noodle soup, it always helps me feel better. You need to eat all of it."

"Thank you, Olivia" He finished the rest.

Olivia ordered herself a bowl as well and sat next to him and ate hers. This soup is delicious. "Are you feeling any better?"

"A little. I'm so tired, I can't keep my eyes open." Gabriel laid back down.

She pulled the quilt over him. "It's best you sleep as much as you can to help your body fight this off."

Once Gabriel fell asleep, she searched online again, hoping to discover more information on Gregory Hanson. She didn't find much more. What little had been reported only led to more questions in her mind? Too bad she didn't know someone who specialized in this sort of thing.

Maybe Gabriel's fever would break tomorrow. She wanted to do more treasure hunting before she left. She must talk with him concerning the flight to Denver. If he'd agree to go, she'd have to support him until he learned enough to find a job. He wouldn't want to leave and she couldn't make him. This left her feeling discouraged. She turned on the TV, hoping to escape for a while.

Chapter Nine

Olivia sat in front of the mirror putting on her makeup. The oatmeal, scrambled eggs, and bacon she'd ordered for breakfast had arrived a few minutes ago. She looked across the room at Gabriel as he woke from the delicious smells. A pot of coffee brewed and she could hardly wait to take the first sip. Gabriel tasted it the day before and loved it.

"How are you this morning, Gabriel? Would you like some coffee?"

"I'm much stronger." Gabriel stood up and headed toward the bathroom. "I might be able to go to the beach today."

"You look better." Olivia opened the drapes and sat in an armchair. "I'm glad you want to get out of this room."

A few minutes later, Gabriel returned and sat in the chair beside her.

Olivia uncovered a dish and placed a plate of eggs and bacon in front of Gabriel. "There are some things we should talk about. My ticket to fly home to Denver is for tomorrow. I'm going in what is called an airplane. You might describe it as a very large mechanical bird. I've checked to see if there is a seat available for you, and there is, but I'd need to reserve it right away."

"We can't leave here." Gabriel leaned closer to her.

"There is no other choice. I don't have a job here. Without money, we can't pay for a place to live or food to eat. My work is in Denver. I only came here to search for treasure. Gabriel, listen to me. You can't stay here alone. You haven't been taught how to survive in this age."

Gabriel stopped eating his oatmeal. He raked his hands through his hair. "If I can prevail against warships and pirates, I can find a way to survive here."

"The way of living we've been experiencing since arriving here is not normal. I've been on vacation, which is to say, I've not had to work, or take care of my home, or the myriad of things involved in my life in Denver.

You have barely begun to see the reality of what you'll need to learn. You're not ready. This has nothing to do with your intelligence or strength. Getting you prepared won't take place in a couple of days. It might be months or even years. You can do it, but not this fast, it's impossible. We can return next year and try to uncover the time portal so you can go back if you still want to." Olivia wanted to cry, and the food had lost its appeal.

"I wasn't created to live in this age, Olivia. I'm only here because of you. Like you, I want us to be together, but if you won't go back, then I will accept it. If I had been born in this age with all these comforts, I doubt I would go back to a time without them." Gabriel stood and walked over to the window. "We're married, but God wouldn't hold us to the vows we made, due to the circumstances. I battled with this yesterday before I became sick, and I don't believe He would fault us if we chose to stay in our own time."

"God doesn't care, but I agree with you otherwise. In your world, you are an important man with duties. In this world, you are lost. Even though my family is gone, I experienced many of the same emotions when I traveled to your time." Olivia pushed her plate and bowl to the middle of the table. "I can't stay in Florida, but, we can look today. I will make a reservation for you. I can cancel it last minute if we need to, but in good conscious, I can't leave you here alone."

"Okay, if we can't discover the way back to my time today, I'll fly on the mechanical bird with you to your home. There isn't any other choice." Gabriel slipped his feet into his flip-flops. "Let's get going, we need every minute of what's left of the day to locate the hole which opens up in the sand."

Olivia breathed a sigh of relief, knowing he'd leave with her if it came down to it. "You should shower first. Then we'll go.

~

"Gabriel, you need to get on the boat." He stopped scanning the beach and walked toward the dinghy. It was being held in shallow water by Jake and a couple of other guys from the Florida Treasure Hunters team. The larger dive boat named the 'Sea Reaper' was anchored just offshore.

Gabriel climbed in. Oliva watched him. He appeared hesitant as he stepped into the fiberglass boat with the outboard motor. After boarding the 'Sea Reaper' he settled down. The inboard motors started with a growl, and they took off for slightly deeper waters. Gabriel looked the part of a sea captain, majestically standing with his long black hair blowing in the wind, gazing at the horizon as the dinghy bounced off the waves. He glanced at Olivia with a smile "I miss sailing and never dreamt a ship could be like this."

The boat engines slowed and then reversed as they arrived at their destination. The anchor dropped into the crystal clear water, and snagged the ocean floor, securing the dinghy from drifting. They watched as the dive team suited up. She decided not to dive, she needed to stay on board with Gabriel. But she was full of anticipation, hoping they'd uncover a relic from the Spanish ships, or better yet, fragments of Gabriel's ship, the *Santismia Trinidad*.

The sun continued to bake them with its intense rays as the day moved on. Dive after dive had produced nothing. The last dive today was underway, after they came up the group would be heading in. Jake was with the team of divers who just went down. Fifteen minutes later he came up yelling with excitement. He'd found something. He gave it to the ship's historian, who carefully examined the find. It was the hilt of a Spanish sword. Gabriel inched closer to get a better look at it. Suddenly, his whole demeanor changed, and he turned and sat on the bench seat.

"It's the handle from my sword, Olivia. I lost it during the shipwreck." His hands shook and Olivia steadied them with hers. "I'm sorry, Gabriel."

This was so strange. Why on this day, of all days, would they discover a part of Gabriel's sword? A coincidence? She didn't think so.

They were puppets on a string. Someone wanted

them to believe they had choices when they didn't?

"Yes! What a find!" Jake held it up for everyone to see. "We could make hundreds of dives and not discover anything like this. You should consider this a special day. This belonged to a man who yielded his sword and possibly his soul to the sea. Or he may have survived but always missed the sword he lost."

"I have a suspicion he survived," Gabriel murmured.

"He could've even captained one of the ships?" Olivia said, playing dumb. Her comment brought mumbling from everybody as they considered this possibility.

"Interesting idea, Olivia. I can't wait until we can better examine it for any type of identification marks that may establish the status of its owner." Jake wrapped it in a piece of cloth and put it in a plastic bag. "Ok everyone, get ready to return to shore." He opened a locked trunk and set the sack in it.

Olivia whispered into Gabriel's ear. "Don't you think it's more than coincidence that they would find your sword handle today?"

"I had the same thoughts."

Olivia hadn't shared with him her online research. He wouldn't understand how. When they returned to shore, Gabriel seemed unhappy and didn't want to look around. Olivia wasn't sure what was going through his mind, but she thought he'd spend every minute of their last day seeking to find the portal.

Back at the hotel, they went up to their room. "Are you positive you aren't wanting to search?" Olivia opened the door.

Gabriel laid on the bed. "I need to rest. Whatever I

had yesterday seems to have come back."

Olivia checked his temperature with the digital thermometer she'd purchased. He was warm, so she got him a cup of water and the medicine.

"Thank you." He swallowed the pills and turned over.

Olivia laid next to him. She felt sorry for him. He must be thinking the situation was hopeless. Seeing his sword handle covered in barnacles, brought home the fact Gabriel and his family had been dead for centuries.

She laid her hand on the back of his head. "I'm sorry Gabriel, I never wanted this to happen. There isn't a believable reason as to how we got caught up in this nonsense."

"It's not your fault." Gabriel turned over, Olivia's hand now rested on his cheek.

Gabriel looked hesitant. "Do you ever think about being married to me?"

"So much has transpired, I haven't had time to." Olivia couldn't decide whether to remove her hand or leave it.

Gabriel touched her cheek. "I meant what I said, no matter what age we're living in."

Alarms sounded inside Olivia's head. Time to bail, too close, you don't want this, but his touch silenced them all.

"I know you did, but I wouldn't hold you to it. You couldn't see what might be in store." Olivia closed her eyes.

"You don't have to ask me to do what's right. I made a covenant with you before God." Gabriel's fingers traveled to her lips and traced their outline. Shivers coursed through her body. "Your cheek and eye are turning purple. I'm so sorry you were attacked."

"The fault was mine for leaving the shelter after you told me not too," Olivia whispered.

"It doesn't matter. You are a lovely woman, Olivia." Gabriel leaned toward her. "I

want to be your husband." He said as he touched his lips to hers.

Time lost all importance. Olivia moved closer. She'd never experienced feelings like this before. She ran her fingers through his hair while she laid beside him. As their kiss ended, she sensed he was waiting for her reaction.

She pulled his head toward hers and kissed him. It was the encouragement he needed. Gabriel kissed her with tenderness and respect.

"Are we ready for this to go any further? We're both torn between two different times and unsure of what we want." His words squelched any further kissing.

"I'm sorry. I wish I wasn't, but you're right. Could either of us be happy in each other's time? We should probably go to the beach and see if we can get you home."

They walked hand in hand to where they had landed. They covered every inch again, winding their way across the beach, searching for the opening for hours.

Olivia sat on the beach. "Gabriel, let's go back. We need to get up early in order to make it to the airport in time."

"I have to search. You can go back. I'll be fine." Gabriel picked up a long stick and started jabbing at the sand.

Olivia glanced up at him. "The facts point to this portal thing having something to do with me, so if I'm not here, nothing will happen. So that means I'll be here until you decide to stop." Olivia was rapidly forgetting what they'd shared a few hours ago. She had no desire to go back in time again.

Gabriel continued. Hour after hour dragged by, with nothing happening. Olivia had even fallen asleep for a brief time, laying on the sand while he searched.

"Gabriel, it's not working, we need to leave. We'll be back next year."

"I can't give up yet, Olivia. My family needs me."

"What if we can't locate it? There are no guarantees. We don't know how or why the portal opens." Olivia stood up and walked back and forth in the sand. "We can search this beach every night for the next fifty years and never get a chance to return to your time again."

"I can't stop trying." Gabriel knelt in the sand and started digging with his hands. "I said I would leave with you tomorrow if nothing transpires."

"Now, you are going to dig your way back?" Olivia laughed, but still got on her knees to help him. Before long, a big hole took shape.

Gabriel pulled out something from the sand and stared at it.

Olivia watched, not recognizing what it might be. She watched him as he sat there looking at it.

"It's my grandmother's ring on my mother's side. I had it with me in the shelter. I had put it on a chain around my neck." Gabriel slid it on Olivia's finger. It was a perfect fit.

Olivia stood up. "That's it. Somebody is orchestrating all these things as if they see what we'll do before we do them. There's no other explanation. Let's go."

"I'm sorry. You'll have to leave me here. I said I would go with you on the mechanical bird, but I can't. I need to be here, trying to find my way back home."

"Gabriel, you're making no sense. The portal won't work without me." Olivia pulled on his arm. "Listen to me. You can be happy here at any given time. It won't be easy, but we'll find a way."

"I'm not a child. I'm a Captain in the Spanish naval fleet. Here, I am nobody. I am led around like a dog. What kind of life is that?" Gabriel glared at Olivia, not moving.

"What happened to your little speech? I will keep my commitment to you? I should've seen you're no different from any other man."

Gabriel flinched at her words as if they had struck him.

Olivia continued. "Listen to yourself. How will you survive here?" She found herself yelling. The man was infuriating. She saw a couple of people looking their way, so she quieted her voice.

"I can get a job with the treasure hunters."

"Oh, it's just that easy, huh? Where would you live, what would you eat? How will you explain your lack of understanding about matters that every person in this age knows? Olivia sat in the beach grass while Gabriel paced back and forth, dragging his long stick in the sand.

It was dark now, and she didn't want to stay out any later. She felt trapped. If she was truthful, she was scared the portal would open up, and she'd find herself back in the year 1715. The longer she remained waiting, the more upset she became. She understood why Gabriel needed to return, but why was he putting her in this position. She didn't know what to do, or what she could do. She asked him to stop. Her frustration was at peak level, so she stood up and ran at Gabriel, tackling him in an effort to make him quit. "We're going to the hotel. I can't take this anymore."

Gabriel lost his footing when she hit him, falling backward with her on top of him. They never landed on the sand, though, because they just kept falling.

"NOOOO!" Olivia screamed.

Chapter Ten

Gabriel rolled over, wiped off his face, and spit sand from his mouth. Olivia was nowhere in sight. Did she follow him through? The thought of her being left behind upset him. He stood and looked in every direction. Not far away lay the Indian his men had shot before they fell into the future. But no sign of her.

"Olivia, where are you?" He shouted.

Nothing.

He strode from the dunes toward the water's edge. The butterflies turned into hawks, gnawing at his gut. Surely, she didn't land in the ocean.

"Olivia!" Again silence greeted him.

Gabriel crouched and stared at the ocean, contemplating living without Olivia. Even if he'd been stuck in her time, at least they'd be together. He came back, but alone. He had never examined the extent of his feelings or what it might be like without her until now.

Waves loudly crashed offshore and the heat of the Florida sun brought beads of sweat to his brow. Inside, his gut clenched in fear. What went wrong? She fell through the portal with him. While traveling through time, there was no noise, only darkness and the sensation of falling. He didn't know when she left him. He prayed.

An abrupt slap to his shoulder made him jump. "Guess we're back where we started before you came to my time."

"Olivia, where have you been?"

"I fell, then I landed behind you. This time, on my feet." She looked at the sky. "Why!?"

Gabriel stood. "I've been here for quite a while. Where did you go?"

"I don't know. I remember falling with you at the start, then nothing until I landed here." Olivia looked out toward the water. "Where did I go?"

Gabriel took her hand. "I thought I'd never see you again."

"I didn't want to come back to this time. I believed you'd learn to like being in the future. When we fell, I tried to roll off you, away from the hole, but it failed." Olivia stepped away, pulling her hand from his. "I wanted you to stay in my time."

"I know you did, but what kind of man would I be there?" Gabriel stared into Olivia's eyes. "You'd be taking care of me. My pride wouldn't let me live like that."

"Now I have the same problem you had in my time. I don't know how to live in this age and you'll expect me to travel to Spain with you, giving up any chance I had of returning. Do you recognize how dependent I am on you here?" Olivia bit her bottom lip. "If something happened to you, what would I do? How would I survive? I am as vulnerable, if not more so in your world as you were in mine."

"I realized this after seeing the future. There's no easy or right answer, but I promise I'll take care of you.

You must understand I didn't bring us back here, it was triggered by you. I'd wandered the beach for hours with nothing. Then you became upset and ran at me. That's when it took place.

Look at how we're dressed. We can't be seen in these clothes. We'll need to go behind the dunes and get off the beach to make our way back to camp. Come with me." Gabriel grabbed her hand.

He led her through the woods back to their shelter. As they watched from the underbrush, men around the camp started yelling. "A small boat is rowing ashore."

"We returned later than the time we left, but not by much." He whispered to Olivia. "Remember, a ship had been spotted before we fell through last time."

"All the men are distracted by the boat coming ashore. Now's our chance to get into the shelter and out of these clothes." He tugged at Olivia's arm. "Let's go."

Chapter Eleven

Loud laughter woke Olivia from her slumber. She'd only planned to rest for a few minutes, but must've been asleep for a few hours. She walked to the door and peeked out into the darkness. If Olivia didn't know better, she'd think the men were celebrating. But celebrating what? They were gathered around a big fire. Outside the wind whipped, and the air in the shelter had a chill to it. Who knew where Gabriel had gone.

She put on one of the dresses Louis had found for her. The gown she had left in now hung in her hotel room. The style of this dress suited her taste more, and she could get dressed without assistance. She pondered whether to look for Gabriel. Last night they'd slept in a comfy bed, tonight it would be the sand with a few ragged blankets and lots of bugs. Olivia decided to leave the shelter and make her way to the fire.

A man she hadn't noticed before approached her. "Where have you been hiding?"

"I haven't been hiding, I've been sleeping. I'm chilled, so wanted to get close to the fire. Did you come ashore from the new ship?" Olivia pointed toward the ocean. The warmth seeped into her skin and took the chill away. The man resembled Gabriel.

"I did Senyora. I'm Captain Manuel Rodriquez at your service. We left Nassau Baja mar when we heard our ships had sunk off the coast of Florida. We're here to recover as much of our valuables as possible and transport the men back to Spain. There will be more boats heading this way once they hear of the possibility of recovering treasure. Pirate ships, that is. Where did you come from, Senyora?"

"I see you've met my new wife, Manuel." Gabriel stepped out of the shadows without Olivia having noticed.

"Your wife, brother?" Captain Manuel looked closer at Olivia. "Maybe you should treat her better as it looks like she took a pretty good hit to the cheek and eye. Not exactly behavior expected from a new husband. Our parents will find your marriage… well, how should I say this? Surprising."

Olivia hadn't even considered Gabriel had siblings. No wonder Manuel resembled him. He did say his last name was Rodriquez. The tension in the air had become thick enough to slice. *Why had Gabriel's brother not been on one of the other Treasure ships in the fleet?*

"A few Indians attacked her. We found her in time to save her, but not before one of them hit her. Thank you for the confidence in my husband's abilities. I suppose our marriage will cause quite a stir." Gabriel put another log on the fire. "I refuse to have my decisions made for me and be used as a pawn to strengthen our relationship with France. You should be pleased to see me fall from favor, as it allows you to take my place and fulfill father's wishes." Gabriel slapped his brother on the back.

"I expect you've wanted to marry the woman they arranged for me, anyway."

Olivia gasped. Gabriel had never mentioned he had been forced into an arrangement to marry a woman from France.

"Why marry what I've already had, big brother. I won't make her my wife nor fulfill father's wishes. The sea is my life. I'm not ready to get married." Captain Manuel smiled at Olivia. "We are neglecting your lovely bride. How did you two lovebirds meet?"

Gabriel's face had turned red. "It's a long story. She's a survivor from one of our ships. She is the only woman here, and the men were harassing her. It made her life miserable and frightening. I offered to protect her by marrying her, and she agreed."

"No offense, brother, but your crewmen like to talk. Two days is not a long time to know someone before marrying them." Manuel smacked Gabriel on the back.

"Olivia, would you mind if I spoke with Captain Manuel? Alone." Gabriel's eyes didn't leave his brother.

"Where should I go? I came out to get warm, it's cold in the shelter. I've never built a fire."

"I'm sorry, I should've asked Louis to make a fire for you. I'll do it." Gabriel took hold of her hand and escorted her through the men.

She wanted to pull her hand away from his because she was upset. He didn't leave the beach when she asked and because of that, she had gotten angry and now they were back in his time. Now, to make it even better, she learns his parents had arranged a marriage for him.

When they got to the shelter, Gabriel built a small fire, taking the chill away. "I'll have Louis bring you something to eat. I should be back soon. How are you doing?"

Olivia moved closer to the fire. "I'm not happy and it would have been nice if you'd told me you were promised to marry someone."

"I didn't think it mattered. I married you, so I can't marry someone else. If you need me, send Louis. He'll stay with you while I'm gone. Manuel's ship is stocked with a lot of supplies. We'll have some decent food tonight." Gabriel walked toward the shelter door. "I'll talk to you later."

Well, she had been dismissed. Olivia took off the gown she'd put on and got into her sundress. It was considerably more comfortable. Louis brought them food, and they ate together. She missed room service, although this dinner had been delicious.

"Gabriel informed me about what went on." Louis began. "How he rescued you from Indians, and then you both fell through a hole in the earth into the future. Your time. Three hundred years forward. I found it hard to believe, but Gabriel is not crazy and wouldn't lie to me. Besides, he showed me the clothes he wore when you returned."

Olivia was comforted that Louis finally believed where she came from. They continued to chat about what had happened, as well as the tension she observed between Gabriel and his brother. After Louis left, she laid down and tried to go to sleep, but only tossed and turned. Her mind kept replaying what happened before they fell through the hole again. She had hoped to be home for good, only to be trapped in this age again. *How would she survive?*

Eventually, her emotions and the experiences of the day exhausted her, and her eyes closed.

Chapter Twelve

Gabriel watched as they loaded the last of the recovered treasure onto his brother's ship. Soon, they'd be returning to Spain, and for the first time, he felt apprehensive about heading home. He wondered if he'd captain any more ships. After what had happened to the fleet, getting back on board had been daunting. He hid his thoughts, but imagined most of the men had similar ones. Some of the men would be staying in Florida to continue looking for valuables and to keep others away.

The storm which had killed so many men that he'd sailed with for the last seven years was more powerful than any he'd ever been through. Pieces of his ship littered the coast, and the stern stuck up in the shallow water just offshore. He expected to see more of the other ships when they started their voyage back. Why had he survived when so many had perished? There was not an answer to this question, only God knew.

Spain was in financial trouble and needed the treasure from the fleet after the war they'd been fighting. But now, most of it lay at the bottom of the sea, strewn along miles of the Florida coastline, with no hope of recovery. He'd never want to live here, too many bad memories.

He hoped Olivia could be happy in his time and he'd never have to come back here. His patience would be tested on the six to eight-week voyage home with his brother at the helm. He wondered if Olivia would get seasick. As usual, he'd be praying for a safe voyage.

His family in Spain wouldn't be pleased he'd married and went against his duty, but he would not leave Olivia here at the mercy of this unsettled territory. Savage Indians wanting to protect their land, and the certainty of cut-throat Pirates on their way to take as much treasure as they could find made it a dangerous place. They couldn't wait around and hope the time portal might open. They needed to go immediately. If she didn't get on the ship, he'd have to carry her onboard for her safety.

He admired her strength and beauty, but the trials they'd have before them wouldn't be easy. He needed Louis to teach her how to fit into Spanish society and what his family and others would expect from her.

~

"Captain Rodriquez, everyone's onboard now. We're ready to set sail." Antonio called out.

Gabriel took one last glance at where they'd lived since the storm. In terms of beauty, this coastline rivaled some of the best areas he'd seen, although no one could survive, it was uninhabitable.

There would be other boats on their way to continue the search for the treasure, but they were a few weeks out. Spain needed to recover as much of it as possible.

Louis and Gabriel had been able to persuade Olivia to board the ship. Although she was distraught, she realized she'd never survive this unsettled territory without the protection of men she could trust. He assured her that his father would be sending new ships every few months to continue in the recovery of their lost coins and valuables. Spain had to maintain a presence here to defend its property.

Gabriel, Antonio, and his brother Manuel boarded last. Louis and Olivia were waiting for them on deck. Her eyes were red and her cheeks blotchy. Gabriel felt bad for her. She was leaving her chance to go forward to her time. He'd almost had to do the same thing. Had they not fallen through the portal, he would've been traveling to Olivia's home in Denver today.

"Louis, Mrs. Rodriguez, and I will be in the first mate's cabin. You'll be staying in the one next to us."

~

Gabriel opened the door of his cabin to see Olivia emptying the contents of her stomach into a bucket. They'd been at sea for a few hours. He had wondered how she'd be doing. He should take her on deck to get some fresh air.

"How are you feeling, Olivia?"

She glared at him. "Obviously, not great. I hope I'm not like this all the way to Spain?" She wiped her mouth with a piece of cloth.

"Let's take you on deck and see if that helps." He extended his hand to her. "Sometimes the fresh air can make you feel better."

Olivia took his hand as he helped her to her feet, too

weak to let her frustrations keep her from his support. He tucked her hand next to his elbow and led her to the deck. He led her toward the front of the ship where she looked straight ahead. The sun was bright, and the seas were smooth with only a small breeze blowing. As they walked by the crew, he saw their eyes follow Olivia.

"Does this help?"

Olivia nodded. "So far."

"Good. I'll have Louis escort you up here when I'm busy so you don't have to stay below deck. I've asked him to teach you what will be expected of you as my wife." Gabriel smiled. "I'll be around to assist him as much as possible. Can you dance?"

"No. I've never had any reason to learn. Even if I had, the dances done in my time would be of no use in this age." Olivia closed her eyes and lifted her face toward the sun, letting the breeze blow across her cheeks as she drew in a deep breath.

"It would be better if you keep the fact you came from 2015 to yourself. Only Louis and I know the truth. We will say you are a sheltered and privileged English woman who had traveled to Cuba with her father to visit friends. He had taken ill while there and passed away. You needed passage back to England, but nothing was available except the ships heading to Spain. So rather than wait for an English vessel to arrive in Cuba, you figured you'd sail with us, and then pay for passage on another ship to England. We met after you survived the wreck of your ship and wandered north searching for other survivors. During the time you stayed with us, I became your protector as there were no other women in our camp. I married you as a form of safety and later saved your life after being attacked by the Indians.

Gabriel glanced at his wife and watched tears run down her cheeks. *His wife*, those words, still seemed foreign in his thoughts.

He placed his hand on her shoulder. "Olivia, I want to pray for you, and for us, if you will let me."

"If you need to, but I don't believe praying will accomplish anything. God just doesn't listen." She wiped tears from her cheeks.

He leaned closer and put his arm around her "I trust God's listening."

Gabriel poured his heart out in prayer, asking Jesus to be their protector, to keep Olivia from being sick as they sailed, and for her to adapt to living in Spain. When he finished, he noticed the tears had stopped.

"You pray as if you're speaking to your best friend. I've never heard anyone pray that way before." Olivia tucked some stray strands of hair behind her ear. Even though she had braided it, the breeze worked parts of it out.

"I was seven when Louis told me who Jesus is, and how much He loved me. I committed my life to Him that day. Since then, I pray at various moments during the day."

"I wanted to sail the seas since I turned ten, but I'm realizing that part of my life may be over. I've encountered many storms at sea, but I'll never forget the terror of that storm." Gabriel stared forward. "So much death. Seeing men who have been part of my crew for years sink into the ocean or wash up on the beach forced me to hold it all inside. I had to be strong. I've struggled to keep it from my mind, but the picture will forever be there."

"Why didn't God save your ships?" Olivia

whispered.

"He has a reason for everything He allows. Why did some of us survive and not others? What could be the purpose of allowing this? We all make choices. Setting sail from Cuba when we did, was foolhardy. Storms are said to be more frequent and stronger during this time of the year. We knew it was risky, but the urgency to get this treasure back to our country made us take a chance we may not have otherwise.

God is always good. He'll bring blessings from this. I love Him come what may, but I won't lie and claim that life is not hard. I have to remember He loves me and He loved every man who perished in that storm. Their deaths won't be in vain." Gabriel took a step back and could see she was feeling better.

He was happy she listened to him, but something in her eyes told him she was not convinced, which made him sad. He had feelings for this woman. He wanted her to know God like he did, she was his wife after all. At best, she tolerated him and at worse, she resented him for being the catalyst that forced her back to this time.

A dark cloud settled over them and he took note of the warning. If their relationship was meant to be, chances were it would demand sacrifice. He hoped that sacrifice didn't cause him to remain true to his words and lose this woman forever.

The sea looked endless. There would be time to talk during this voyage.

Chapter Thirteen

Olivia went down the planks to the dock. When she stepped onto the dirt, she breathed a sigh of relief. The first solid ground she'd stepped on in seven and a half weeks. Louis walked beside her with Manuel and Gabriel behind her. Antonio had glared at her as she walked across the deck. She wouldn't miss being around him. The man gave her the creeps. She heard he would be leaving on another ship.

A few days into the voyage, Manuel fell and broke his arm, preventing him from performing his duties as Captain. Because of this, Manuel asked Gabriel to captain the ship. While he was recovering, Manuel offered to assist Louis in teaching Olivia about the Spanish culture and the responsibilities and expectations of being a princess.

Being Captain of a Spanish merchant ship took up all of his time, which caused Gabriel to be away from Olivia except for meals and when he slept.

She worked during the days with Louis and Manuel. She enjoyed learning about the customs and traditions that living in Spanish civilization afforded.

She still had much to remember but hoped she had

a small grasp on what life in 18th Century Spain might be like and what would be expected of her.

Olivia followed Gabriel and Manuel toward a carriage that would take them to Gabriel's home. Gabriel opened the door and offered his hand. She almost tripped over her dress as she grabbed his arm and wedged into the carriage. Getting in and out of narrow spaces wearing these wide dresses would take practice. They traveled a short distance and stopped.

"This is where we'll be living, this is my home. Manuel has offered to tell my parents the news of our marriage. I'm positive they'll be quite surprised."

Manuel shut the carriage door after they exited. "I'll send you a note, brother." He then winked at Olivia. "And don't worry Olivia, you'll be fine."

Olivia glanced at Gabriel. His face turned red.

Gabriel took Olivia's hand. "I can take care of my wife, brother, now that I don't have to run your ship. I'm still amazed at how well your arm is now, it's as if it was never broken." He said as they turned to walk toward the house.

Manuel leaned toward the carriage window. "This conversation with our parents should be exciting. I'm sure I'll see you both very soon."

Louis had already arrived and was waiting for them outside the front door. He greeted them and they walked up the steps of Gabriel's home, which was now hers too. A rounded arch framed the front of the house. It was a nice-sized home, but with Gabriel being the King's son, she expected it to be larger. "You don't live at the palace?"

"Occasionally I stay there, but I have my house now. I had it built not long before I left on this last voyage." Gabriel opened the arched wood door. The detail work on it was amazing. The interior walls were cream-colored with gold trim. The vaulted ceilings were covered in mural paintings of clouds, sky, and angels. A curved staircase led to an upstairs balcony, overlooking the marble tiled floors.

"This is beautiful." Olivia touched the walls as they walked through the hall into the kitchen where the servants were talking. When they saw Gabriel, they stood at attention.

An older man approached him and bowed. "Infante Gabriel, Your Royal Highness, we were not expecting you."

"Juan Carlos, may I introduce to you my wife, Her Royal Highness, Princess Olivia. Olivia, this is my el mayordomo, my butler."

"Pleased to meet you." Olivia greeted the servants as Gabriel introduced them.

"Juan Carlos, please have your staff prepare lunch for us. Also, her Royal Highness, Princess Olivia will be needing some new clothing. Can you have the carriage brought around after we finish lunch, so we can visit the dressmaker?" Gabriel took her hand and led her to the dining room.

"Servants stood alongside the dining room table, with chairs already pulled out, waiting for them to be seated. A huge crystal chandelier hung over the table. After being seated, it wasn't long before multiple plates containing bread, olives, cheeses, pork, lamb, chicken, and rice, were put in front of them. One goblet was filled with water, the other with wine. She enjoyed the food, although it was somewhat spicy.

As they were near the end of their dinner, Juan

entered the room. "Your carriage is ready, Infante Gabriel."

"Thank you, Juan." Gabriel wiped his mouth. "We're about finished."

"Olivia took one last bite of chicken and a sip of water. She could've eaten more, but she was excited to visit the dressmaker."

"When we return, we'd like to bathe and then have dinner." Gabriel took Olivia's hand, and they left. Outside, the carriage which waited for them was not as elaborate as the one that brought them here, but it was nice. Gabriel had been subdued at lunch and also on the ride into town. She sensed he was tense. When they arrived at the dressmaker's shop, Gabriel introduced her as his la mujer, wife. The surprise on the dressmaker's face was obvious, even though she tried to recover quickly.

Olivia was measured then moved to a dressing room where she tried on numerous gowns, cloaks, shoes, and undergarments. She left with four gowns, a couple of day dresses, and chose four more styles they'd sew together. She had new shoes and every undergarment she could need. Way more than she required. Why was everything so uncomfortable? She just wanted her jeans and t-shirts. Her heart hurt. Not only was she in another time, but she was thousands of miles from Florida with no chance of going back soon.

Gabriel sat in silence while they rode in the carriage. He was courteous and cordial with the dressmaker, but since they'd left, he'd said nothing.

Olivia couldn't remain quiet any longer. "Is something wrong, Gabriel?"

"What do you mean?" He didn't look at her, he just

continued staring out the window.

"You've hardly spoken two words to me since we got to Spain."

"I have a lot on my mind."

"Would you mind sharing? I'm alone in a strange place." Tears welled up in her eyes.

"I assumed you were upset with me."

He turned and looked at her. "I'm responsible for you being here, remember?"

"Yes, I'll admit I want to be upset with you, but I realize you're the only one I have here who knows who I am.

Gabriel went back to staring out the window. "You didn't tell, Manuel?"

"No, why would I tell him?"

"Well, you both seem to be pretty friendly." Gabriel showed no emotion as he spoke.

"I only had him and Louis to talk to. You were always busy."

"I had to Captain the ship, remember? We would've never made it to Spain had he been at the helm. He tends to avoid responsibility whenever he can. He'd much rather be around women, in pursuit of his next conquest." Gabriel turned and glanced at her again. "So how did he fare with you?"

"How dare you." Tears slipped from Olivia's eyes. "He kept me sane with all his silly stories and taught me things I needed to know before we got to Spain. Louis was always with us. Nothing happened that anyone would consider unbecoming for a married woman." Olivia wiped her tears away.

"I doubt he thinks your attention is that of a friend. I can tell he considers himself my rival for your affections. It's always been that way with him, if someone has something then he'll want to take it from them so he can feel superior. I love my brother, but I do not like who he is." The carriage was slowing and Gabriel looked out the window. "We're back. I am ready for a bath. I should not have said that." He helped Olivia out, and they walked inside.

Juan was waiting for them. "I'll have your clothes brought up, Princess Olivia. Please, follow me upstairs." He led them into a massive bedroom with a beautiful stone fireplace and a huge canopy bed.

"I'll have hot water and perfume brought up for your baths."

"Thank you, Juan." Gabriel shut the door as he left.

"Everyone expects us to be sleeping in the same bed. We don't want any rumors getting to my parents." Gabriel kept his back toward her.

"We've been sharing the same bed since we married. I am sure I can continue." Olivia peeked into an adjoining room where two tubs sat side by side. She assumed not many people had this luxury. She understood she needed to count her blessings. At least she wasn't in a peasant's cottage in the early 18th century. She couldn't imagine how difficult her life might be in those circumstances. She was a princess wed to the King of Spain's son.

A few maids carried in hot water and poured it into one of the tubs.

"Fill only one tub for now. I'm letting my wife have the first bath alone." The maids soon came back with more hot water and then some cold. When Olivia got in, the temperature was perfect. She hadn't realized how wonderful a bath would be after so many weeks without.

She had soap and towels. What more did she need?

She laid her head back and contemplated Gabriel's actions today. He must be jealous of Manuel, but he had no reason to be. Olivia knew Manuel was a flirt, and she appreciated his friendship over the last few weeks traveling to Spain. It wasn't fair of him to expect his brother to take over captain duties on his ship. She drifted in and out of sleep as she relaxed, but the water started to cool.

A woman waited for her in the bedroom and helped her dress. The gown they choose tonight was a deep blue and made her eyes stand out. In this age, without much makeup, one had to think of such things. Once finished, Gabriel came in and they got his bath ready.

"What's your name," Olivia asked the maid as she brushed out her hair.

"Maria Gonzalez."

"Thank you for helping me tonight."

"I'm your lady's maid. I'll be here to help you with whatever you need." Maria pulled part of her hair up and pinned a ruffled fabric cap on the top.

"Do all the women style their hair like this?" Olivia wasn't delighted with the look.

"It is very fashionable right now. Do you not like it?" Maria sat the brush on the dressing table.

"I'm not sure, but it will do for tonight." Olivia smiled at her. "Thank you, Maria."

Maria smiled back at her in the mirror. "Will you be requiring anything else?"

"No, I'm fine."

Maria turned to walk out the door. "I'll be back to help you get ready for bed."

"Thank you, Maria."

"You're welcome, Your Royal Highness."

Could she ever get used to these titles? Louis and Manuel had familiarized her with them and their proper use in society. They instructed her of her position in her household, and when she's at the castle. She was intimidated by the thought of staying at the palace.

Gabriel stepped into the room dressed. He must've gotten ready in another bedroom. "Shall we go to dinner? You look lovely."

"Yes, I'm very hungry."

Olivia glanced at him and smiled. He was extremely handsome. She hadn't seen much of him the last few weeks, but all cleaned up he made her heart flutter. In a good way. He even smelled amazing. Something she'd missed since they'd left her time. He seemed to be in a better mood. He placed her hand in the crook of his arm, and they went down the stairs and into the dining room where Louis waited for them.

"I must say, the two of you make a most handsome Royal couple." Out of respect for their titles, he waited for them to sit first.

"Why thank you, Louis I am a hundred times better after my bath." Gabriel took a drink of his water. "I feel like an inch of dirt was removed."

Louis laughed. "It probably was, my friend. I'm thankful we're back safely in Spain." He glanced at Olivia. "The Lord has been good."

"Yes, I'm glad we're safe and grateful we missed any storms and turbulent seas on the way here. My stomach wouldn't have survived it." Olivia sat back as a bowl of soup was placed in front of her. "Is it spicy, Gabriel?"

Gabriel smiled. "You should be safe."

Dinner was delicious and the conversation never ceased. It'd been the most relaxed she'd been since coming back to this time. Louis was like an uncle to her. It was easy to see why Gabriel loved and respected him.

The sound of the door knocker interrupted their laughter.

Juan soon appeared with a note from the palace and handed it to Gabriel.

"My parents expect us for breakfast in the morning. I knew they wouldn't wait long. I guess we should prepare for battle. Would you pray for this meeting, Louis?"

Louis proceeded to pray over them for protection, favor, wisdom, and boldness. A peacefulness enveloped her when he finished.

"Well, we better get some sleep so we can be refreshed in the morning." Gabriel walked over and pulled Olivia's chair out. "I'll let you know how it goes, Louis."

"I'll be anxious to hear." Louis took the last bite of his roll.

Olivia rose from her seat. Do these people ever finish a meal? She'd barely made it through half of her main course. She had hoped to eat dessert. She snatched a slice of bread to take with her as Gabriel took her other hand. Both of them were silent as they walked to their bedroom.

Maria was waiting for Olivia when they opened the door. Good Evening Princess. Gabriel walked into the other room. She helped her get out of the many layers she had on and into her nightdress. It had rows of lace over the deep blue satin and accentuated her figure in all the right areas.

Maria took the pins out of her hair and brushed it out. Olivia had never been one to be pampered, and she wanted to do this herself, but she'd been informed by Louis that wouldn't go over well.

Maria sat the brush down. "Is there anything else you may need?"

"No, thank you again, Maria." Olivia smiled at Maria as she closed the door. Gabriel soon appeared from the other room.

Olivia went to the bed and drew back the blankets. "Everyone knows how all this goes except for me."

Gabriel laughed. "We've been doing this much longer than you have, although I must admit adding a wife to my routine has altered things." He put another piece of wood on their fire and blew out the candles, leaving only an oil lamp dimly burning by the bed.

"I hope that will be a good thing for you. This house is absolutely beautiful." Olivia glanced around the room. It was decorated in shades of blue. Light blue drapes hung at every window, while darker ones surrounded their canopy bed. A mural was painted on the ceiling of a ship at sea with a village in the distance. He must have had it done to represent him coming home to Spain. The bed was enormous, with carvings on each wood pillar. As gorgeous as everything was, the fireplace is what stood out to her as being the most elaborate. She remembered seeing pictures of castles and palaces and thinking of how grand they were. Gabriel's house was a smaller representation of that.

He laid down, turned away from her, as was his habit. Then he prayed. The only time it had been different was in Florida when they'd shared a few kisses. Since then, he hadn't acted like he wished to get near her.

She scooted closer to him, not quite touching, but close enough to gather warmth from his body. She didn't know why she'd made this move. Maybe because she was tired of being alone. Maybe because she wanted to see if he was as immune to her as it seemed. Or maybe she just needed to be his wife before facing his family, knowing they'd try to tear her from him. Without this man, she had no way back to Florida, ever. She'd be on the streets having to do unspeakable things to survive.

Olivia rested her hand on the back of his head and ran her fingers through his hair. She scooted even closer and wrapped her arm around him. He twisted toward her.

"Are you cold?"

"A little." Olivia shivered. To be truthful, it had to do more with being next to him than being cold.

He turned his head away from her again.

Was the man daft? Did he not understand she was offering to him what she'd never offered to any man before? She didn't know what to do, she didn't want to make a fool of herself. She should sleep. Tomorrow would be a long and emotional day. She had no doubts from everything which had been said. She struggled to fall asleep, but being this close to Gabriel stirred emotions inside her. He was her husband, and these feelings were normal. Olivia kissed his shoulder.

She'd finally gotten his attention, and he turned over into her arms.

"Do you realize what you are doing?" He cradled her face with his hand.

"Yes."

Gabriel smoothed her hair back out from her face. "This is what you want?"

"Yes, I wish to be your wife." Olivia stared into his

dark brown eyes. It was hard to discern his emotions.

Gabriel continued looking into her eyes. "Olivia, you're already my wife. If we never came together as a married couple normally does, you would still be my wife. I don't think you realize how much you've come to mean to me. Jealousy ate at me for weeks on the ship until I could hardly stop myself from punching my brother. I've made a covenant with you and with God and I intend to honor it." He kissed her forehead.

"But I'm only your wife in name. They will try to take you away from me as we have not fulfilled our marital duties. They won't consider our marriage valid. I studied history and I know how this goes." She tried to smooth out his furrowed brows with her finger. "I want to honor the words I spoke to you by being a wife to you in every way."

"Do you only think of this as a marital duty? I can wait for you. I want you to love me or at least have strong feelings for me. I don't want this to be a duty." Gabriel gently kissed her cheek. "No regrets."

"I have feelings for you, Gabriel. I have never been in love before, but the emotions I have inside for you are like nothing I've ever known. I want to be the one you share everything with. I need to meet your family knowing we have a real marriage, and that we're building a stable marriage, whether we remain in your time or mine. I have doubts about being in this time, but I don't have doubts about how I am feeling. Do you even desire me?" Tears pooled in her eyes.

"I didn't want to push you. It's hard for me being so close to you every night and pretending I'm immune to you being there. I told God I would do it for as long as you needed. My commitment to you will not be any greater if we take our marriage forward. It's not based on that. You've also said you resented me for bringing you back to this time again, and I understand. I just want it to be right." Gabriel wiped a tear that had escaped the corner of her eye.

"I realize I've held things against you, but it's been hard. I understand none of this is your fault, nor mine. I need to belong to you, to be closer, to know our marriage is real, not just a form of protection for me but that you want me for your wife." More tears escaped. She had never been more vulnerable than she was now.

"I desire nothing more, Olivia. I want to share my life with you, have children with you, and get to know every aspect of you. I wish for us to be together when our hair turns gray. I want us to be in love in a way I've never seen. My parents had an arranged marriage and my grandparents and I see them tolerate each other and at times there is love, but I don't see a passion for each other that outweighs everything else. I need that with you, my wife. From the moment I saw you, you had my attention." Gabriel kissed her gently, lovingly.

Her heart melted from his words and his touch. She had found a prince among men, and she longingly kissed him back.

He drew her closer into his arms.

Tonight she'd learn what it meant to be loved by her husband, Gabriel Matias Rodriquez, heir to the throne of Spain.

Chapter Fourteen

Gabriel helped his wife into the carriage. He couldn't have been more surprised by the unexpected turn of events last night. God must be answering his prayers to forge this marriage into one of love. He never expected to care about a woman as much as Olivia. Their time had been filled with one setback after another, but yet it looked like they were meant to be together. She still wanted to return to her life, but he prayed that would change.

Gabriel held Olivia's hand as he slid in beside her. "How are you this morning?"

"Imagining I'm on my way to the lion's den." Olivia smiled. "I hope reality turns out better."

"I feel the same way. I'd love to say you're mistaken, but knowing my parents, you're probably right." He kissed her cheek. "We'll face the lions together."

"So much for making a girl feel better." Olivia squeezed his hand. "I suppose this day was inevitable."

"Did I tell you how lovely you look today?" He kissed her neck.

"Maybe a couple of times, but a wife can never hear that too much." Olivia kissed him back.

"And a husband can never get enough of those." Gabriel caressed the side of her face.

The carriage came to an abrupt stop, almost causing them to tumble into the empty seat in front of them.

"What is going on?" Gabriel leaned out the window. "A deer ran in front of us. I see it leaping into the woods.

They sat in silence the rest of the way. His wife was uneasy. When the carriage came to a stop in front of the palace, he realized he was just as worried.

"Looks like we're here, Olivia. Let's both take a deep breath."

"Oh my, this is way beyond anything I imagined."

The carriage door opened, and a footman helped Olivia out. Gabriel followed. The palace doors were open for them. His parents and siblings stood inside the great hall to receive them. Manuel stepped forward, smiling.

"Here's the happy couple." He kissed Olivia's hand, holding it longer than he should. "Hello, brother."

His mother hurried to hug Gabriel. "We're so relieved you're alive and not hurt. The loss of men and treasure has been devastating to our country. What a blessing God spared your life and Manuel was in the area and brought you home."

Gabriel kissed his mother's cheek. "I'm also thankful. Mother, here is something else I'm especially grateful for. Let me introduce you to my wife, Princess Olivia. Olivia, this is my mother, her majesty, Queen Elenor."

"Manuel told us the news of your marriage." The

Queen grasped Olivia's hand in both of hers. "We're pleased to meet you, Olivia."

Olivia curtsied. "Thank you for your hospitality and welcome, your Highness."

"Let's not stand on ceremony this morning, it will make it easier for Olivia, right Philip?" She smiled at Gabriel's father as he joined them.

"Yes, we're very happy to meet you, Olivia." His father smiled.

"Thank you. I appreciate you welcoming me into your home." Olivia's voice sounded shaky.

"Why don't we talk over breakfast, we can finish the introductions then." His mother led the way to the dining room.

Gabriel placed Olivia's hand on his arm as they followed the procession. "We've survived the initial lion encounter. He chuckled as he kissed her cheek.

"I've been able to take a couple of deep breaths so I didn't pass out." Olivia smiled.

As they walked down a hall, complete with statues and marble floors, the smells from the awaiting food made Gabriel's stomach rumble.

Olivia was seated between him and his brother. Gabriel assumed Manuel had a hand in the seating arrangements. As their food was being served, the conversation was slow. Olivia trembled beside him, so he held her hand to help calm her nerves.

His mother sat straight across from him. "Gabriel dear, how did you two meet?" She took a bite of her scrambled eggs.

He wondered what and how much Manuel had told them. It was a bad idea to let him give them the news. He needed to be specific with his story, as well as letting them see his affection for Olivia, so they'd recognize how important she was to him.

"Olivia wandered into our camp after surviving the wreck of the ship she was on. She was the only woman who made it that we are aware of. I took her under my watch with Louis as a chaperone to protect her.

During our weeks on the Florida coast, we encountered many risks and didn't know if we would live from one day to the next. As the highest-ranking officer, I offered to marry Olivia to provide her a better chance of staying safe. She reluctantly agreed.

Louis married us and it is legal and binding. Since then, I've protected her, even saving her life from an Indian assault. We've continued to grow closer and are now in love. I made vows before God with her, and I have the utmost confidence we'll enjoy a long and happy life together." Gabriel smiled at Olivia, then kissed her.

His mother looked at Olivia. "Were you married before?"

"No."

"That is true mother, she had never been with a man before me," Gabriel stated. He saw Olivia's face and every woman's face at the table turn red.

"You should've saved that conversation for another time." Gabriel's mother choked on the water she had taken a drink of before he spoke.

Manuel slapped Gabriel on the back. "Well, brother, I didn't realize your relationship had progressed so fast. Congratulations are in order, I see."

"We're finished with this questioning, so can we speak about other matters?" Gabriel squeezed her hand under the table.

Gabriel's father glared at him. "You do recall that

you were already pledged to a woman in marriage, don't you? You had no right to marry Olivia, no matter the reason."

"I see we're not ready to move on. Yes, I remember, but circumstances demanded a different outcome." Gabriel took a drink of the milk in front of him.

The King sat back in his chair. "She's on her way here to demand you honor your arrangement with her."

"I'm already married and I won't relinquish my marriage to Olivia. Princess Elisabeth is not a woman I would want as a wife, even if I didn't have Olivia. You made this arrangement Father, not I. There are many things I've done for my country, but this will not be one of them." Gabriel held his own in the discussion.

Manuel chimed in. "Her father won't be happy at this turn of events. I'm not sure what he'll do."

Gabriel slapped his brother's back harder. "You should wed her, Manuel, since she already knows you so well. In fact, she is acquainted with you in ways I never was with her. What's the difference between brothers after the eldest and heir apparent, anyway? We're just pawns used for our country's bidding."

"Gabriel and Manuel that is enough! Gabriel, you will meet with her. It's the right thing to do. If Manuel wants to marry Princess Elisabeth, your father can arrange it." Queen Eleanor stood and everybody followed.

King Phillip turned to talk with Gabriel. "I'll inform you when the Princess arrives. We'll be having dinner in her honor. I need to talk to you in private about all that's transpired. Olivia, you're welcome to leave. I hope you'll understand. I'll have a carriage brought around."

Gabriel noticed a tear escaped Olivia's eye before

she wiped it away.

"We're taking a walk before I meet with you, Father." He took her hand and led her into the castle gardens. "I'm sorry, Olivia. I knew it would not be easy."

"It's not your fault. As a King's son, you had obligations before I dropped into your life. I just never expected to be ignored, dismissed and intimate details exposed in front of people who are now my family, but yet strangers.

"This is why I thought it better for us to stay in the future. My family is gone. Explaining your presence in my life would've been easy. I'm positive your family is assuming I am a peasant who was seeking to marry royalty." Olivia broke down sobbing.

Gabriel pulled her into his arms and whispered into her ear. "Olivia, we must be cautious of our discussions here. There are spies all over the grounds who report everything to my parents."

She wept even harder. He held her until she calmed. "This won't be easy and if you can't do it, I'll take you back to Florida. We'll go to your time if we can." Gabriel wiped her tears away with his finger. "When I told my family that we've fallen in love, it wasn't just to enhance a story. I may not have been talking for you, but I was speaking for myself. I've truly fallen in love with you, Olivia."

She studied him. Her brown eyes glistened with unshed tears. "I promise to try, Gabriel. You love your family and your country. I've already caused enough turmoil. You are a vital part of what takes place in Spain. I hope my presence in your life has not altered this."

Gabriel picked a perfect red rose next to them in the garden and put it behind her ear. "I think your presence here only makes my life increase in value. I'll be home as soon as I can. My father wants me to describe every detail as he records it. When you get back, ask Louis to show you around the property so you're not sitting alone in the house on this beautiful day."

Olivia rested her head on his chest. "I will."

He drew comfort and strength from her being so close. He heard a dog barking not far away and assumed his father had sent someone to get him. "Let's go. The carriage is probably waiting." They strolled hand in hand to the front of the palace. Olivia climbed in and he closed the door and waved as they moved out of sight.

Time to face the King. The battle lines were drawn and his father did not give up easily. After finding out every detail of what happened the night of the storm, his attention would inevitably shift to manipulating Gabriel into marrying Princess Elisabeth.

Chapter Fifteen

Olivia woke to an empty bed. Gabriel had not come home. *Why did he stay at the palace?* If they lived in her time, his cell phone would've been lit with text messages and calls. She rang the bell for Maria to help her get ready. Olivia asked her to check if Louis could join her for breakfast.

When she walked into the dining room, Louis stood up from his chair. Their meal was served as soon as she seated herself. The staff was exceedingly efficient at attending to her every need.

"Would you know why Gabriel didn't come home last night, Louis?"

"I'm not positive, Princess Olivia, but my hunch is they had company arrive and persuaded him to stay." Louis coughed and took a drink of water.

"Company, as in, Princess Elisabeth? How convenient to have sent the wife home." Olivia cut into her ham like she was killing the pig.

"I can simply speculate at what transpired, but I'm confident it was not what Prince Gabriel wished to do."

Louis tapped his fingers on the table in succession.

"Why are you so certain? He could've come home had he wanted to." Olivia sat her fork on the napkin. She no longer had an appetite.

Olivia stood. "Is there someplace I can go to look at shops? Who would I take with me?"

"Yes, I'll have the carriage readied for you. Maria will accompany you. I can also go if you want me to." Louis stood out of courtesy to Olivia.

"If you believe it's safe, I'm fine going with Maria." Olivia glanced out the window behind Louis. It looked to be a pleasant day outside.

"I'll inform the driver to take you to town. Maria will know where to go." Louis grabbed another biscuit from the bowl.

"Please, Louis, eat your breakfast. Just because I'm not hungry shouldn't mean you need not finish. I'll go to my room and wait for Maria to call on me." Olivia faked a smile.

"Very well." Louis sat in his chair and continued eating.

Olivia walked out of the room and made it to the stairs before tears flowed down her cheeks. Why hadn't he let her know why he didn't come home? The King had told them that Princess Elisabeth should be arriving soon. The more she pondered it, the more her sadness changed to anger. She entered their bedroom and sat on the window seat.

She watched the servants going about their activities outside and she felt an ache grow inside of her for her former way of life. Back home, she had significance and purpose. She taught history and volunteered in many things. Here she was an ornament or an instrument to produce children. Here, the husband had as many mistresses as he wanted, while the wife waited for him at home.

She heard a tap on her door. It was Maria. "Princess Olivia, the carriage is waiting. Are you ready to go?"

Olivia grabbed a light shawl to take with her. "Thank you, Maria, and thanks for accompanying me today."

"You are welcome. I like going out." Maria smiled.

"I'm sure this trip is a welcomed break for you. We'll have to do this more often so you can get out of the house once in a while." They went down the stairs and out the front door into the cool, crisp morning air. Olivia drew a deep breath and glanced around. The leaves were turning to fall colors. The footman helped them into the carriage. They rode in silence until they reached town.

"You're familiar with all the shops, I assume?" Olivia asked.

"Yes, I have not been inside many of them, but I do walk through here a lot." Maria stepped down.

"Good, show me the shop you find the most fascinating." Olivia chose to exude an air of confidence and hope for the best.

"Princess, I cannot walk in front of you," Maria whispered.

"Of course, well, just point in the direction we should go." Olivia needed to slow down and recall what she'd been taught concerning protocol.

Maria pointed to a bakery. When they stepped inside, the aroma of freshly baked bread filled Olivia's senses. It reminded her of her grandma and the times she made rolls for them. She went over to the case which was filled with so many wonderful desserts, she had a hard time choosing. She picked a chocolate crème pastry. They walked across the street with their sweets and sat on a bench to eat them. When they finished, Olivia noticed a family giving away puppies.

"Maria, look at the puppies! Let's hold one." Olivia quickly made her way to the family, Maria followed behind her.

"May I hold one? Olivia asked."

"Of course." The mother handed her a little brown and white fur baby.

Olivia was in love. She glanced at Maria. "Should I get it?"

Maria was smiling ear to ear. "She's so cute! I don't see why not if it would make you happy?"

She'd always wanted a dog but had never been able to have one. Could anything truly make her happy? At least she wouldn't have to be alone in that big bed. "I think I will."

Olivia thanked the family and took the puppy. They went back to the bench and let her run around their feet.

"Well, I would've never guessed I'd run into my favorite sailing companion."

Olivia jumped and turned her head. Manuel stood behind them.

"It looks like you have found a cute distraction." He picked up the pup, and she covered his face in licks.

Olivia laughed at the puppies' affectionate reaction to Manuel. "I have. But I'm realizing I don't know what a puppy needs or where to get it."

"Is your carriage nearby? I can help you with that." Manuel sat the fluff ball down.

"Just so happens it is." Oliva pointed across the road

where the carriage waited.

"Good, we'll take it down the street." Manuel offered his hand. Olivia took it and got up from the seat.

She scooped up the puppy, and they strolled to the carriage and got in. Manuel took them to the local livery where he commissioned the saddler to make an intricate leather collar with engraved scrollwork and a leash.

"Thank you for helping us, Manuel. I've never had a dog before." Olivia cuddled the sleeping pup in her lap as they rode back into town.

"Well, I'm glad you do now. My brother will be delighted." Manuel paused. "If he ever makes it home to meet her."

Olivia had wanted to ask him where Gabriel was but didn't want to be the one to bring it up.

"Hopefully, my parents and Princess Elisabeth will remove their claws from him soon. She keeps delaying the meeting so he can explain to her she's free to find another. It's not hard to recognize her scheme, at least for me. The woman is shrewd." Manuel winked.

"Hopefully, Gabriel is wise to her ways." Olivia stared out the carriage window.

"If he is wise, he'll return to the charming woman waiting for him at home." Manuel patted her hand.

Olivia found his touch disconcerting. She feared there might be another manipulator nearby. The carriage slowed to a stop.

"This must be where I say Adios. Thank you ladies for allowing me to accompany you this afternoon. Good day." Manuel jumped out and waved goodbye as he strode up the street.

She decided it best to return to the house so the puppy could get used to her new home.

Olivia glanced at Maria. "What should we name her?"

"Names are always hard." Maria folded her hands in her lap. "Maybe wait until you see more of her personality."

"What a wonderful idea. Thank you. I've appreciated your company today." Olivia sat back in her seat.

"I am glad to help." Maria rubbed the puppy's head.

Olivia wondered if Gabriel would be there when they got home. If not, she might have to show up at the palace uninvited.

Chapter Sixteen

Gabriel couldn't believe he was still at the palace. He should've left yesterday, but his father was adamant that he wait for Princess Elisabeth to emerge. She was in the castle but kept delaying the meeting. Her lady's maid said she was so upset that it's made her ill. Gabriel didn't believe the excuse. He knew how manipulative she could be. He was positive she was deliberately keeping him there and away from his wife.

His parents informed him that the King and Queen of France had threatened to punish Spain financially through a trade war if this marriage arrangement didn't occur. His father reminded him of the desperate state of their country's treasury after losing the gold and valuables they gathered from Mexico. It now rested on the floor of the ocean. Spain needed this alliance with France.

He was leaving by nightfall, whether she spoke with him or not. His father would need to soothe things over after that. He'd not waste another night away from Olivia.

He wandered through the gardens, trying to keep his anger in check. His sister, Francesca, walked with him.

She had tried to find out more about Olivia's past and who her family was, but Gabriel stuck to the plan, not divulging anything. He was sure his parents had put her up to it.

"Well, brother, I am going back inside."

"Thanks for your company, I'll be in shortly. Gabriel watched his sister head across the manicured lawns. He worried she wouldn't give up. He slowly walked toward the balcony which overlooked the gardens. Princess Elisabeth came out from the palace about ten feet in front of him.

Gabriel approached her. "I hope you will talk with me now."

"Is that any way to greet the woman you're supposed to marry? Your lifelong friend who's spent every summer with you since we were young children?" Elisabeth stepped closer and laid her hand on his chest.

Gabriel stepped back, letting her hand drop from him. "Our parents agreed to this marriage to forge a stronger union between our countries. But life has a way of changing things we didn't plan on. I'm my own man and choose not to be bound by their decisions. I am aware that you've made plenty of irresponsible choices with other men who were not to be your husband."

Elisabeth stepped closer. "You know that many royal couples are not faithful to their marriage, it's almost expected of us. I only need your title and what that will bring to my country. You can keep your soon-to-be mistress around to visit."

"She'll always be my wife. I will not marry you. This was bound to happen anyway, as I cannot be wed to a woman who won't be faithful." Gabriel stared into her brown eyes.

Elisabeth touched his face. "I find such a statement baffling as I understand she prefers Manuel to you."

The remark struck him where he was most vulnerable. He struggled not to show a reaction but realized Princess Elisabeth's smile meant she knew she had accomplished her mission.

Gabriel moved her hand from his face. "You heard wrong."

"Am I interrupting something, brother?" It was Manuel who had appeared out of nowhere.

"Not at all. I was just leaving." Gabriel glanced at his brother.

"You'll find a pleasant surprise when you get home. I spent the afternoon with Olivia and she was wondering where you slept last night." Manuel smiled.

Gabriel was reminded of how much his brother and Princess Elisabeth were made for each other. "Well, now you two can spend the evening reminiscing over your previous experiences together. I'm going home to my wife."

He wouldn't take the bait Manuel dangled in front of him, anticipating he'd ask what surprise was awaiting him. He just turned around, walked away, and didn't look back. He headed straight to the stable where his horse was boarded. The long ride home would hopefully clear his mind after contending with the two of them.

~

Gabriel opened the door to his house. He had a lot of explaining to do. He should've never bought into the manipulation that kept him at the palace. He foolishly expected the meeting would be quick and everything would be settled. Instead, it turned into a twenty-four-hour nightmare. Elisabeth may be a princess by birth, but he wanted no part of her life. He silently thanked God for protecting him from her.

The house was quiet, so he went upstairs. Olivia wasn't in the bedroom, so he asked Maria where she might be. She said Olivia was in the gardens.

Olivia was sitting in the grass with a tiny puppy running around her. That must be the surprise. He leaned down and scratched the pup behind its ear. "What have we here?"

"A new addition to keep me company when my husband doesn't recall where his home is." Olivia glanced up at him.

"He remembers, and He's sorry. He forgot that some individuals can never be trusted. I hoped to get matters worked out but instead was reminded I'm only a pawn in a chess match. No one cares what my opinion is, just that I do whatever it takes for the good of the country." Gabriel sat in the grass across from Olivia.

She tried to get the puppy to let go of her sleeve. "I assume that means I'll be your ex-wife?"

"No, I told them you're my wife and that will never change." Gabriel loosed the puppy's grasp on her sleeve.

The puppy crawled into her lap and closed its eyes. "What will the princess do then?"

"Go home, I hope. She's not wanted here, at least by me." Gabriel smiled at the adorable furball. "So what is the puppy's name?"

"I don't know. What do you think is a good name for her?"

"Hmmm. How about Maggie or Bella?" Gabriel noticed Louis heading toward them.

"I like Bella, that's a cute name."

"Louis, look at our newest family member? Olivia decided we needed a guard dog." Gabriel laughed.

"Yes. I've met her, she's quite ferocious. I hate to put a damper on the good mood, but a message was delivered from the palace." Louis handed a card to Gabriel.

Gabriel scanned what it said. "Looks like we're being summoned to the palace tomorrow night. Princess Elisabeth's parents are coming and want to talk with me. I can't refuse. They'll try every loophole to say our marriage is invalid. We may need you to testify to them, Louis." Gabriel watched Olivia's face.

She sighed. "What do want at this point?"

"A lot. They aren't ready to give up." Gabriel handed the note to Louis.

"They sound serious. I'll go with you." Louis handed the card back to Gabriel.

"We should talk about what they may try to do, Louis."

Gabriel glanced at Olivia. "I will see you at dinner."

Olivia cuddled Bella to her. "Of course.

Gabriel followed Louis to the house. He had hoped Elisabeth's parents accepted the changes and it wouldn't go this far. It seemed they were going to try everything in their power to make him marry Elisabeth. He needed to come up with a solid plan to counter anything they might put out. He'd not let them take Olivia from him. He planned to fulfill his words to her. Gabriel entered the kitchen with Louis asking God for wisdom.

Chapter Seventeen

Olivia stepped from the carriage with Louis right behind her. They came together as Gabriel had been called to the palace earlier in the afternoon. Dread consumed her. It grew into a weight, compressing her lungs and stomach with each step she took toward the castle. Breathing became labored. She wanted to turn and flee.

She had no idea what awaited her inside. Could they make Gabriel divorce her?

They walked into the great hall and followed the butler to a sitting room. Eyes shifted to them as they stepped into the room. She felt confident in the way she looked. Maria had taken extra care with her hair and Olivia picked out the gown she liked the best. It accentuated her curves. Well, the best they could be with these styles. The deep plum color made her eyes brighter and added pink to her cheeks. She missed having mascara, though.

Gabriel came to greet her and placed her hand on his arm. "Everyone, I'm pleased to introduce you to my wonderful wife, Olivia."

She walked around the room, greeting each person

individually. After the introductions, they went into the dining hall. Louis had left to eat with the other servants, even though Gabriel didn't consider him one.

The candlelight glistened off the crystal goblets, the china, and the silverware, all the best on display for this dinner. Manuel and Elisabeth sat directly across from Gabriel and her, with Elisabeth glaring at her. The seating arrangements obviously didn't come about by mere coincidence. Everyone ate in silence. She wondered if the tension in the room might explode from not being addressed. She had no idea what food they'd served because she hadn't eaten a bite. The knots in her stomach squeezed tighter.

Manuel broke the silence. "How's the new puppy?"

"Playfully adorable." Olivia smiled.

Manuel took a bite of the roasted meat. "What did you name her?"

"Gabriel liked the name Bella, and so did I." She glanced at Gabriel, but he stared across the table at Elisabeth.

"So brother, are you keeping the dog?" Manuel asked.

Gabriel blinked. "Indeed. Why would we name Bella if we weren't keeping her?" He said as he took a sip of wine.

"I'm glad little Bella is keeping you company, I hear Gabriel hasn't been." Manuel coughed.

"He's been pulled in many directions since we arrived and has tried to be forthright with everyone." Olivia nervously dabbed a napkin to the corners of her mouth. Silence resumed until the last bite. Gabriel's father suggested the men retire to another room. Panic seized her at the thought of being alone with these women.

"Gabriel, I can't be left alone." She whispered in his ear.

He stood with the men as if to follow, but announced, "Father, I won't be joining you."

"Nonsense, the ladies would like to get to know Olivia better without us men around." He smiled at her.

"She hasn't exactly been accepted here, father." Gabriel pulled back her chair.

"Gabriel, we have guests." His mother looked pale.

"I'm sorry, mother, but there should be no pretense here. It's simple. I married Olivia, and I plan on keeping my vows. I'm sorry that changed plans, but the plans were never made by me. I'm sure if everyone was honest, they would understand circumstances happen in our lives that we don't foresee. It doesn't mean those changes are wrong, in fact, they could be for the better." Gabriel touched her cheek. "I love Olivia."

Olivia wanted to flee from the room. Gabriel's words were perfect, but the anger directed toward her made it impossible to relax. She wondered where Louis had gone. He'd make sure she got home.

Everyone stood as the Queen rose. "Come, Olivia, let's listen to Francesca play the piano. No one needs to talk about anything. The men should not be that long."

Olivia's legs shook like Jell-o. She didn't dare refuse to go. She followed the Queen and the other women into another beautiful room. Books lined the shelves on the walls, and a grand piano posed stoically in the middle of the floor. True to her word, Francesca seated herself at the piano and began playing. Beautiful melodies flowed from her fingers. Olivia found herself lost in the music until she realized Elisabeth had left.

What nefarious things could she be up to?

Everyone was mesmerized by Francesca's next song, so she used that opportunity to leave. Olivia wondered through the corridors, having no idea where she was or where her wanderings might lead. She came upon a balcony overlooking the gardens. Golds, pink, and oranges lit up the sky as the sunset. A couple stood together by some bushes in conversation. After squinting to see who they were, she realized it was Gabriel and Elisabeth. How did he get out of the meeting with the men?

They stood very close. Olivia could hear Elisabeth talking but couldn't make out what she said. She looked upset, occasionally wiping her eyes. Olivia looked away for a few seconds, trying to decide if she should make her way down there. When she glanced back, Elisabeth had her arms wrapped around Gabriel's neck, kissing him. Olivia gasped. Seconds ticked by. Gabriel never attempted to move away or get loose from her embrace.

Olivia turned and ran through the chambers until she located the front door. Outside, she spotted her carriage a short way up the drive and hurried to it. The driver stood nearby. "Please sir, take me home."

Manuel stepped from the shadows. "What's the hurry, Olivia?"

She couldn't hide the flood of tears running down her cheeks.

"You're crying. What happened?" Manuel stepped closer.

"I saw Gabriel and Elisabeth kissing." Olivia sobbed. "He didn't even try to stop her."

"Are you positive?" Manuel hugged her to him as she continued to weep.

Olivia lifted her face from his chest. "Yes. Why did I believe this marriage would work? There are too many influences working to pull us apart. I never belonged here."

"So you wish to leave?"

"Yes, I can't handle this."

Manuel touched her hair. "Gabriel told us the whole story. That your father passed away in Cuba while you traveled together visiting friends. He also said you have no family left and were on your way to England. I'm the captain of my vessel and could take you anywhere. However, my father is sending me back to Florida tomorrow to watch over the treasure recovery. I'd return you to England on the way home, but you'd need to go with me to Florida first. I'd keep you safe."

Thoughts swirled through Olivia's mind. *This might be my only way home. Hopefully, I'll find the time portal while in Florida. Otherwise, I'll tell Manuel who I am and how I got here. He could verify it with Gabriel or Louis.*

Olivia realized she was taking a huge gamble. If she didn't find the portal, she'd return to Spain with Manuel. She couldn't go to England.

"I need to keep this from Gabriel. He deserves to be happy with the woman he was expected to marry. I don't want to be in his way. He apparently has feelings for her even though he said he didn't." Olivia was shaking.

"I will see what I can work out. Don't mention this to Gabriel. Act like everything is fine. My father may be able to find an errand to send him on tomorrow so you could get out of the house without anyone knowing." Manuel tucked a few wisps of her hair behind her ear.

Olivia didn't realize what he was doing, she was so

emotionally distraught. She had to leave.

"I'll explain to Gabriel you tried to find him, but you had to go home because you were feeling sick. You'll need to pretend you're sleeping when he gets there. My ship is ready to leave. I will get word to you once Gabriel leaves on this errand." Manuel looked around. "Let me help you into the carriage."

Olivia got in. Manuel closed the door and nodded to the driver to go. He smiled as he waved goodbye to her.

The carriage rattled over the cobblestone drive, but Olivia didn't notice. What she had witnessed made no sense. After everything he had said this evening, then to see him kissing Elisabeth. Did she really know this man? This could be her only chance to get back to her time. Leaving Bella behind would further break her already broken heart. What choice did she have?

Her mind's eye played reruns of Gabriel and Elisabeth kissing. She felt so betrayed. Tears came again and she let them flow. Once she got to the house, Maria would realize she'd been crying. Olivia would tell her she was sick and just needed to go to bed.

The rugged Spanish captain had stolen her heart. She loved him. She'd never been in love before and now understood how badly it could hurt when you felt it being ripped away. Why? Why God do you hate me so much? Gabriel believes you're real, and if you are, you must enjoy seeing people in pain. Yet again, the only person I can count on is myself.

~

Olivia opened the door to her cabin on the ship. She'd be next to Manuel's because he wanted to keep an eye on her. It hadn't been easy leaving the house without any of the servants seeing her.

Gabriel came home late last night, and she had pretended to be asleep. She stayed in bed and let him get up first. He'd hardly gotten up when a note was delivered summoning him to the palace again. He had kissed her on the cheek and explained his father needed him to deliver an important message to his cousin. He'd be gone most of the day. By the time he returned, she should be well out to sea.

She sat down in a rickety chair and breathed deep. Did she make the right decision? Right or wrong, she was headed to Florida. Going there was the only chance of discovering the portal. She missed Colorado, her students, and the life she'd built there. Her family may be gone, but she had friends, well, acquaintances. Anyway, they were better than not having anyone. Being a history professor supported her and allowed her to live a good life.

The prospect of another six to eight weeks on a ship caused her to cringe. Louis or Gabriel would not be with her. She had Manuel, who'd been kind and understanding with her, but something told her she needed to watch him. Gabriel didn't trust him, and even though he said all the right things, she believed his motives were self-serving.

She laid on the bed, which was more like a cot, and struggled to go to sleep. She hoped it would help her from becoming so seasick. She was heartsick. She missed Gabriel, and the realization hit her that she'd never see him again. She abandoned her husband because she couldn't watch him choose the princess. She had thought Gabriel loved her. She'd been wrong.

She turned over on her side. Sleep wasn't coming anytime soon. Olivia needed to train her mind to ignore the questions that had no answers. This would be a long voyage. The ocean must be calm as the ship barely swayed as they left. She wondered if Gabriel had returned home yet and read her letter. Would he toss it in the fire or would he be devastated she'd left? Why did she feel in her gut she acted too hastily?

Chapter Eighteen

"**W**hoa." Gabriel pulled on the reins as he neared the stable. He'd rode to his cousins to deliver the message and returned without stopping. He wanted to get back to Olivia as quickly as possible. He worried she was upset over everything, which took place the last few days. He would be in her place and truth be told, he had some explaining to do.

The afternoon sun felt good in the cool fall air. He jumped off his horse, gave the reins to the stable boy, and ran to the house. Once inside, he yelled for Olivia, but there was no response. Did she go out again with Maria? If she did, she hadn't left a note. He needed to take a bath, so he rang for the maid and informed her of his intentions. She said Olivia left before she came up earlier this morning to make the bed.

He waited while they filled the tub and then sunk his body into the warm water. At least he wouldn't smell bad when she returned. He laid his head on the back of the tub and dozed off. He woke up when the water had cooled, so he hurried and washed. After getting dressed, there was still no sign of Olivia. The downstairs servants said she left early this morning, but they didn't know where she was going.

Gabriel walked outside to look for Louis. He lived in a small cottage on the back of the property. He devoted many hours to the garden, so he hurried his steps toward there. He found him, bent over the raised beds, pulling weeds around the plants.

"You do realize we hired a gardener?" Gabriel startled him.

Louis stood up and wiped his hands on his pants. "Yes, but some things I want to do myself."

"I'm searching for my wife. You wouldn't have any idea where she is?" Gabriel hoped his answer would be yes.

Louis looked around the property. "No. She isn't in the house?"

"No." Fear tried to break its way into his mind, but he managed to keep it at bay.

"That's strange. I saw her this morning at breakfast, but not since. She was a little quiet, but nothing unusual. No one's come by the house that I'm aware of, but I walked all around the property today." Louis patted him on the shoulder. "Did you look for a note or ask Maria? Is the puppy here?"

"I didn't see a note downstairs, and I don't know where the puppy or Maria are. Maybe they left together, but you'd expect the other staff to say Maria went with her. I'm heading back to the house."

Louis yelled, "Tell me what you find out."

On the way to the house, Gabriel found Maria outside with clothes she'd just washed and the puppy running around her. Olivia had told her to take the day off, so she was catching up on her laundry. He quizzed her about Olivia, but she hadn't seen her since she helped her get ready this morning. He went to their bedroom and opened the drawers where her underthings were kept. They were empty. In one drawer laid a folded piece of paper. His heart picked up its pace, and he read the words.

Gabriel,
This will come as a shock, but I am heading back to Florida with Manuel. He is going there to oversee the treasure recovery, but I am sure you've been told this. I understand your commitment to me is not something you chose, in fact, you felt pushed into it in order to protect me.

When I saw you kissing Princess Elisabeth last night, I realized how much my presence has changed your life. You were pledged to her, and the two of you grew up spending time during the summers together since you were children. I didn't wish to create division between you and your family, but it has happened. I expect it will be forgotten once you marry the woman you were destined to.

Manuel will hopefully report to everyone that I disappeared if I can find the time portal. When I get back, I'll return to Colorado and never return to Florida as I never want this to happen again.

When I discovered that I loved you, I realized I could not stay here and share you with another woman. You'd struggle to do the honorable thing, but being pulled between two women would make it impossible for you to be happy.

I wish you would've shared this with me. It left me in shock and so confused.

I'll never forget you and in my heart, you'll forever

be my husband.
Always, Olivia

Gabriel's heart broke. Why did she leave before speaking with him? What she'd interpreted as a kiss between him and Elisabeth was not a kiss on his part. She'd suddenly wrapped her hands around his neck and yanked his head down as she covered his mouth with her lips. The first couple of seconds he'd been in shock that she'd done such a thing. He struggled to pull back, but she tightened her grip around his head. He pried her arms from him in order to move. He told her to never do that again.

When he got home, he intended to explain to Olivia what took place. He should've woke her up when he made it back from the palace, but he worried she'd not believe him. Then he was summoned to deliver an emergency message to his cousin and thought it could wait until he returned. He'd prayed about it on his ride back from taking the note and knew he couldn't put it off. He had to be honest.

He should've told her right away. Obviously his silence played into her perception of what transpired, and of course, his brother just happened to be there to play the hero. He was sure Manuel was out for another conquest, but little did he realize that Olivia was planning on leaving permanently.

He needed to locate a ship ready to sail, and the sooner the better. He raced down the stairs and out to the garden to inform Louis of his plans. He asked him to find out if any boats were equipped to leave and emphasize his need to go right away. He hoped the winds would be in his favor. If he was too slow getting to Florida, she'd be gone, and he'd not be able to get to her.

Gabriel asked the stable boy to saddle a fresh horse. He had to speak with his family. He didn't know how to explain Olivia leaving with Manuel to Florida, but he'd tell them everything Elisabeth did which had upset her. What they needed to accept is that he wouldn't tolerate any more of their games to get him to marry Elisabeth. If they did not bless his marriage to Olivia, they'd move somewhere else and never see them again. Many cousins would be willing to help them.

His heart was heavy. If there weren't any ships ready to sail, it might take days to prepare one for a voyage. In that case, catching them would be… Impossible was the word that came to mind.

He jumped on his horse and took off at a full sprint toward the palace. He needed to pray.

Chapter Nineteen

Olivia could scarcely raise her head from the cot. There was a bucket next to her on the floor. In the week since they'd left, they passed through one storm after another. Even when it wasn't storming, the seas had been monstrously rough. All she did was puke.

She had pleaded with Manuel to take her back to Spain. Olivia realized she'd made a huge mistake in leaving without first speaking to Gabriel. He told her no and reminded her she chose to come. They'd be in Florida until the treasure became hard to locate. He guessed it might be five to six months.

She'd had plenty of time to reflect on that night and what took place. She didn't understand why Gabriel kissed Elisabeth, but she should've let him tell her what had transpired. She had rushed into this trip and regretted it every day. Why didn't she think what Gabriel and she had shared was worth fighting for? If he chose the princess, then she could've asked him to take her to Florida.

Manuel had stayed distant since she had asked to return to Spain. She looked a mess and guessed he didn't want to be around someone throwing up or hadn't wanted to remain with him. If it wasn't for the boy who brought her food and water and emptied her buckets, she'd be alone. And he never spoke, so she only had herself to talk to.

Suddenly, shouting erupted above her. Their words were indistinguishable from everyone yelling. Deafening booms resounded. She felt the ship shudder. She struggled to sit up, but dizziness overwhelmed her and she immediately laid back down. Loud noises and powerful impacts shook her from her bed. They must be under attack.

In all probability, it would be pirates. *Why didn't she stop and consider what she was doing before letting her emotions drive her to return to Florida with Manuel?*

She held her hands over her ears, fear coursing through her body. The ship was making creaking sounds like she'd never heard before, as if it was being ripped apart. Her mind was flooded with thoughts of dying. She thought about Gabriel and his relationship with God. She had only prayed a couple of times in her life, and in those moments He must not have been listening.

The ship rocked back and forth from the explosions, and Olivia wondered how long until it sunk. The noise ceased for a few seconds, then a tremendous thud against the boat sent her bucket spilling across the floor, causing her to gag. She had to get out of this cabin, but where would be a safe place to hide?

"God, please help me!"

She stood up, and the vertigo was gone. She opened the cabin door enough to peek outside. No one was in sight, but there was lots of yelling. She moved into the corridor and tip-toed to Manuel's room. She looked into the unoccupied room. The only place to hide was under the bed, but she needed a weapon. *There has to be something in here, he's the captain.* Olivia went through the drawers in his desk one by one and found a dagger under some papers. Footsteps were walking down the hall. She quickly slid under the cot just as the door flung open.

"I don't know what you're speaking about," Manuel said.

Olivia peeked from under the bed between the blankets hanging down. Two men angrily pushed Manuel into the cabin, then into his desk chair. One of them tied his hands behind the chair back while the other one held a pistol.

"Where's the treasure, captain?" The pirate with the gun yelled.

"We have no treasure," Manuel replied.

The pirate who tied his hands hit Manuel's face, making Olivia cringe.

"I don't believe you!"

Again, the repetitive smack of knuckles against bone filled the air, with Manuel groaning in pain.

Olivia closed her eyes only to open them and see blood dripping off the corner of the chair and splattering onto the floor.

"You better tell us, Captain, you see this knife...?"

Manuel yelled, and Olivia saw the pace of the blood drips quicken. She covered her eyes.

Manuel tried to talk but was having trouble. He choked, then said, "We're on our way to Florida to recover more of our treasure." Manuel's speech slowed, then steadied. "We have nothing on the ship at this point."

"I've never seen a Spanish ship have nothing of value. This vessel is a magnificent prize in itself, but that was before we created several holes in it." The men laughed.

"Since you've established it's of little value, and you can see we have no treasure, what more do you need from us?" Manuel answered.

"I'd still like to keep this ship for myself and you're in my way, captain."

A deafening bang erupted causing Manuel and the chair to fall over backward. He hit the floor with a thud, a couple of feet from the bed, blood pooling around him.

Olivia screamed.

A long-haired dirty man looked under the bed, grabbed her arm, and yanked her out. "What do we have here?"

Olivia screamed again as he pulled her to her feet. She glanced at Manuel, the sight more than she could bear. She had never seen so much blood. "Manuel! No!"

The door opened, and another man strode into the room. "What happened? I ordered you not to kill him."

Tears ran down Olivia's cheeks. Her whole body shook and her heart raced with fear and anger.

"He threatened me, captain. I had no choice." Said the man who shot Manuel.

"Liar!" Olivia screamed.

He shifted his hate-filled eyes toward her and raised his hand to hit her. "Shut up, or you'll be next."

"He was the King of Spain's son. You're an imbecile. Let her go." The captain pulled out his pistol and shot him in the chest after he'd released Olivia. "I told you to never disobey me." He yelled as the man hit the floor.

Olivia started crying. "Please don't kill me!"

The captain looked at Olivia. "Don't worry, madam. I'm sorry your friend is gone. I wish I'd made it down here sooner. I had no intention of him losing his life, he was worth more to me alive, than dead. My men will not be happy to learn their hope for ransom is gone. Let me introduce myself, Edward England, at your service, and you are?"

Olivia was confused by his demeanor. He acted as if they'd just met at a social gathering instead of in a room with two dead men lying on the floor. She wiped tears from her eyes and glared at the man. "Olivia Mendez." She thought it better not to tell him her married name.

"How well do you know this, Captain?" Edward asked. "After all, you were hiding under the bed in his room."

"I'm just a passenger."

"You sounded a little to upset to be a mere passenger on his ship. You called him by name, not by his title." Mr. England studied her.

"My sister is engaged to be married to him in the summer." Olivia hoped her lying words came across as truth.

Edward tapped his fingers on the desk. "You don't look Spanish. Are you married?"

"I'm of English descent, but my husband is Spanish. He's on a boat heading to Florida as well. I had to leave a couple of days behind him as I had commitments to my family. In Florida, I will be helping him document what treasure is recovered from the shipwrecks."

"It seems we both have a vested interest in recovering treasure. I'm sorry for your family's loss, but what's done is done. Your sister will find another, maybe he has a brother."

Olivia tried not to react to that remark.

"You'll be sailing to Florida in my ship. Whether I'll have mercy on you and your husband is yet to be determined, but for now. you're under my protection, and no harm will come to you. If you have any belongings, you need to get them. This ship will be set on fire. I don't wish to leave any evidence pointing to me killing the King of Spain's son. But, you know what took place so it may be hard for me to return you to your husband."

"I promise I won't tell anyone. You have my word." Olivia was looking into a real pirate's face. Growing up, she had read books about pirates and their escapades. She'd watched movies and speculated what it would be like to live in such a time. They portrayed them as handsome, and they stole from the rich like Robin Hood. She now understood they were not Robin Hood and his merry men.

"I haven't gotten this far in life by trusting every woman who has promised things to me. It's strange how wanting to stay alive will let one's tongue run wild." Edward opened the door. "Let's go."

Olivia had to step over Manuel's legs to get out, causing tears to well up in her eyes again. Gabriel and his family would be devastated. *Why hadn't Manuel listened to her and returned to Spain?*

Chapter Twenty

Gabriel scanned the horizon, hoping for a glimpse of Manuel's ship. The winds had been in their favor, and he hoped they'd made gains on his three-day advantage. Louis had located a boat, and it was close to being ready to sail. His father didn't help. He claimed there weren't any vessels available. Gabriel doubted he spoke the truth, as nothing would make him happier than to no longer have to worry about Olivia being in their lives. So he commissioned a private vessel with a paid crew. They charged an exorbitant price for the use of it, but it was the only one that offered him a chance to catch Manuel.

They'd been at sea for roughly two weeks without sight of any ships. Doubts of catching them filled him and he prayed for peace. The first port of call would be Cape Verde. Manuel most likely docked there. Knowing his brother and how he enjoyed indulging in the local debauchery, he probably stayed a few days.

They should reach Cape Verde any day now. The last eight days at sea had been smooth sailing. The weather and wind couldn't have been better. He'd seen dark clouds ahead of them many times, but when they got there they dissipated. He doubted Manuel's ship experienced the same luck. This voyage gave him time to reflect on all the times God protected him. The latest being the storm that sunk their ships.

He pondered the sequence of events that brought Olivia and him together. If he hadn't encountered that storm, he wouldn't have been on that beach when she traveled through time.

He recognized that through the suffering and death that occurred on that tragic day, good came from it. God had allowed them to be brought together for reasons not yet identified. He must have something important in store for them. These reflections produced a new optimism. Because if true, it meant he'd find her.

"Captain Rodriquez, we've spotted what looks like debris from a sunken vessel up ahead." Louis handed him a telescope.

Gabriel extended the scope to get a look. He saw wood timbers and other debris scattered across the ocean. As they got closer, he knew it was wreckage from a ship.

"Captain, there are survivors in the water! One hundred meters to the port side!" An unknown crewman yelled.

"Lower the sails and prepare for rescue!" Gabriel shouted.

The sails were dropped, and the ship slowed. They lowered a couple of crewmen in a rowboat into the water to rescue the four men hanging on to a large portion of the ship's stern. He took out his scope to see if he recognized them. He did. They were crew members from his brother's vessel. Gabriel began to get a sick feeling in his belly as a cloud shrouded the sun above them.

Everyone stood in silence watching the men being

pulled out of the ocean and into the rowboat. It seemed like an eternity before they were rowed back to the ship and climbed up and over the railing onto the deck. They crumpled from exhaustion when their feet touched the surface of the boat.

"Get these men some water and food. Right away." Gabriel commanded.

"Captain Rodriquez, we have never seen a more welcome face. It's been a nightmare." One of the men held out his hand.

Gabriel recognized this crewman and helped him up. He'd went through the storm with him and survived. His insides grew tense and the hope he'd known just hours ago faded. "Carlos, what happened to you? Whose ship were you on?"

"Your brothers, Captain Manuel Rodriguez's boat. Pirates attacked us and then set fire to the ship, after killing many on board." The man took a long drink of water from the flask they brought him.

"What happened to my brother? My wife, Olivia? My understanding is she had come aboard as a passenger?" Gabriel wanted to shake the man, why did he have to drag this out of him.

Carlos paused, his face distraught. "I'm so sorry to tell you this, Captain, but your brother is dead. One of the pirates shot him. I heard they took your wife captive aboard the pirate ship."

Gabriel was screaming in agony on the inside, but he had to find out more. He spoke to another of the surviving crewman. "What about you? I don't believe I know you. Do you know anything more about my wife?"

"Sir, my name is Thomas. I've sailed with your brother many times, but never with you, Captain."

Thomas took long gulps of water from the almost empty flask. "They killed most of the crew during the attack on our ship. The few of us still alive were left to burn or go down with the boat after they set it on fire. As they sailed off, I do recall seeing her aboard the pirate's vessel."

"Do any of you know the pirate captain's name?" Gabriel had heard reports of these pirates. They had no regard for life and enjoyed torturing and murdering people. Did Olivia tell them who her husband was?

"I believe they addressed him as Edward England." Carlos struggled to stand and this time made it to his feet.

"Thank you men for your service to my brother and the King. Louis, I'll be in my cabin, if needed." Gabriel turned and strode away.

Gabriel slammed his cabin door shut. He bent over, put his hands on the desk, and drew a few deep breaths. Anger boiled inside him. He wanted to yell and break something. His brother was murdered and his wife taken captive. What would this pirate do to her? How would he find her?

"God! Why?" He yelled. He needed to repay this pirate captain in full for what he'd done to his brother. If he hurt Olivia, they'd locate him and kill him no matter how long it took. Gabriel slammed his fist on the desk.

Vengeance is mine, Gabriel. I will bring justice.

The words played through Gabriel's mind. "I can't wait for your justice, God. I demand it now." He walked over to his cot and slumped down onto it.

Trust me.

"I did. Why did You let my brother be murdered? I don't know if my wife is alive. Why would you allow that God?"

Silence. No more words played through his head.

Anger marched through his body, causing every vein to swell and feel like it would burst. He flipped the table over as he stood up and raced out to the deck. "Louis, furl the sails, we're continuing toward Cape Verde. I'm expecting this pirate, Edward England to be there. He is going to wish I never crossed his path."

Louis rested a hand on Gabriel's shoulder. "I know you're upset, but you need to pray for wisdom in how to locate Olivia and protection when confronting these pirates."

Gabriel shrugged it off. "I don't have time to pray. God didn't have time to save my wife and brother."

"I realize you're angry and hurting, Gabriel," Louis whispered. "Don't do anything you will regret for the rest of your life. You have to be in command of your thoughts. Running on anger might get you killed."

"I appreciate you trying to help, Louis, but I have to do this my way. God's way didn't work. My brother is dead, and Olivia has been kidnapped and possibly violated or worse." Gabriel's thoughts suddenly returned to how thankful he had been to God earlier today. Why was He punishing him? He'd always tried to do what God asked of him, but apparently, it hadn't been enough. He must require a far greater sacrifice than Gabriel was able to pay.

Chapter Twenty-One

Olivia looked over the railing of the pirate ship, gazing at the infinite body of water in front of her. She must admit the freedom she'd been allowed on the vessel bewildered her. Not one crewman talked to her in any manner, but respectfully. For a pirate, Edward England, was either lulling her into a false security, or he indeed did what he said.

He'd not attempted to make any advances toward her. They ate their meals together, and he remained courteous. Their conversations traveled in many directions. She constantly guarded her words. She didn't want to divulge information that might generate suspicion or cause him to guess her ties to Spain's royalty.

Olivia often experienced flashbacks from the attack on Manuel's ship, and the horrific violence she witnessed. But she also remembered crying out to God for help, and He answered. Her seasickness had miraculously disappeared, and Edward kept her safe when she had wondered if they'd rape and kill her.

The cruelty and killing that day had been so pointless. She'd seen the ruthlessness and lack of empathy Edward England displayed when crossed. He became a terrifying man, *Dr. Jekyll, Mr. Hyde*.

A younger boy, looking to be in his early teens, approached her and discreetly handed her a piece of paper. He whispered. "Miss Olivia, I need to tell you something. Before boarding this ship, a man I'd never met before pulled me aside and informed me a woman would be captured and taken aboard this vessel. He said her name would be Olivia and that I must give her this note."

Olivia took the sealed note and immediately pushed it down the front of her bodice. "That makes no sense. How did this man know what would happen? What did he look like?"

"He looked like everybody else, dirty and poor, but he paid me generously. I must go before I get whipped." The boy darted off as quickly and quietly as he'd snuck up on her.

Olivia stood in disbelief.

Edward walked up to her. "I saw my cabin boy speaking to you. You look upset. Did he bother you?"

"No, he asked me if I needed some water. He reminded me of my youngest brother and talking to him made me homesick." Olivia smiled with sad eyes. "I remembered all the love we shared. Nothing better than family."

"Awe, yes, I have heard Spain is a beautiful country. You mentioned your grandmother came from England. Where is home?" He raised one eyebrow as he posed the question.

Olivia anticipated he'd eventually ask about her heritage. She needed to keep track of what she said so he couldn't call her out on a lie. "My mother's grandmother was English. I've been told I resemble her. I am not sure of her name or where she lived as my mother ran away at a young age and never spoke much about her family."

"Surprising that it showed up so far down the lineage. Maybe there were more secrets you are unaware of. Your mother may have found another man with whom she had dallied with. A fine Englishman such as myself." He stared out to sea.

"I suppose anything is possible. Although, my mother loved my father dearly." Olivia glanced at him. *Time to change the subject.* "Do you have a wife in England?"

"I do. A beautiful wife who I've loved for ten years. Unfortunately, she's s very sick and I lack money to get her the medical help she needs. I did not wish to leave her after the war, but I had no other choice. Her sister is taking excellent care of her." Edward coughed.

"I'm sorry, how terrible for you." Olivia wanted out of this conversation, but couldn't come up with a way to do that and not insult him.

"I am sure you consider me a heartless man, but I am not. I forced myself to be unaffected by death in the war, after having to kill so many or be killed, otherwise, I might have gone insane. Lives will be lost, there is no other choice.

My men only want someone who will do what it takes to make them rich. To show any type of compassion or weakness would lead to a mutiny. They only leave you alone because they understand you are mine. If something happened to me, you'd not be so lucky." Edward stared at her. "I suspect there is much more to you than you have led me to believe."

"Land, Ho." A crewman yelled.

"Sounds like we've made it to Cape Verde. Time to go ashore. We need to re-supply the ship. Stay in your cabin while I decide whether it's better for you to remain onboard or if I'm taking you with me." Edward turned and strolled away.

Olivia breathed a sigh of relief as she walked to her cabin. The man couldn't be accused of being a fool. The paper stuffed in the bodice of her dress poked her skin every time she moved. She needed to read it. Back in her room, she pulled out the note and opened it.

Olivia,

I realize you must have many questions. But the biggest is sure to be - How did you come to be in the 1700s? My name is Gregory Hanson, and I'm a distant cousin from the mid-nineteenth century. I consider myself a scientist, and I invented a time machine that allowed me to travel to different eras. It is not a vehicle in that you get in it and go, it's much more complex. I will spare you the details.

The initial time I crossed into another age, I traveled forward to the year 2015 and landed on a beach in Florida. I passed through the portal just before you fell into it. It was quite unexpected for you to be at that place at that exact moment, and even more so when I discovered we're related.

I panicked and realized you needed back to your time. I discovered a way for you to trigger the portal, but yet be unaware of doing so. My second mistake was in allowing Gabriel to pass through with you.

It took many trips between your 2015 and 1715 to figure out what would happen if certain scenarios played out. I discovered Gabriel needed to stay in his time. However, in order for him to get back, you had to go with him. I programed the portal to open when you were in the area and you were upset, it refused to let anyone go through without you.

I'm continuing to work on providing you another chance to get back to your age. Whether you take it or not will be up to you.

I assume you've discovered that when you go back or forward in time, you pass through to the same date and time as when you left. Even though I invented this, I don't have all the answers. I am sorry to have interfered in your life. I didn't thoroughly understand the consequences of what I hoped to accomplish.

My advice to you is to follow your heart. I hope to be in touch soon.

Your cousin, many generations removed,
Gregory Hanson

Olivia didn't believe what she just read. It made sense, but yet it made no sense. Even if she sailed to Florida, she might not be able to travel forward. She shoved the note back into her bodice, folding it smaller. The knowledge that there may be no way to go to her time caused her to panic.

She paced the cabin and pondered Gregory's words. She needed to find a way to escape. She'd need to persuade Edward to take her ashore. If she did get free, how would she find a way back to Spain? Olivia didn't have any money to book a passage, and these islands crawled with pirates who wouldn't be as gracious to her as Edward England had. From their last conversation, she sensed he suspected she might be of more value than he originally assumed.

A brief nap might help. She needed to have a clear head to devise a good plan.

Chapter Twenty-Two

Gabriel, Louis, and a few of his men rowed toward the shore in two small boats. They'd anchored just offshore from Cape Verde. There were many ships moored at the island which served as the last stop on the way to Havana and Mexico. He hoped the pirate Edward England and his pirates were here. He expected to find out. Thick dark clouds were on the horizon, warning a storm might blow in. He'd been here many times, but never with this much rage churning his insides.

He couldn't pray. He wouldn't pray.

They pulled their boat onto dry land and headed for the most popular tavern. If Edward England was here, someone in there should be aware of it. They sat in the shadows and watched men drink their earnings away. A couple of guys came over to their table and pulled out some chairs. They apparently recognized his crew.

Gabriel's mood was foul, and he wanted to hit someone. It didn't matter who, it would just feel good to release some of the anger which rolled over him in waves.

"Hey, Captain, this guy said he saw England yesterday. He doesn't think they've set sail yet."

"Are you aware if they're staying on their ship or in town?" Gabriel asked the man.

Hope flickered for a moment.

"I'm not sure, captain. He was in here last night with his crew. They got into a couple of fights with some locals. They always cause trouble."

"Thanks for the information." Gabriel handed the fellow a silver coin, then motioned to his men. "Let's see what we can find around town."

Gabriel looked in every direction for a glimpse of Olivia as they wandered up and down the streets. No one they asked recalled seeing any of them. Either everyone was scared of crossing him, or he kept his dealings very secret. Even his men must keep silent about what they planned.

They walked to the harbor, and no one admitted to seeing him. Darkness was settling upon them, so he and Louis decided to get a room. He ordered his men to spread out around town and ask questions, especially in areas of drunken depravity and prostitution.

~

The crowing of a rooster roused Gabriel from his sleep. He'd only gotten a couple of hours of rest. They'd soon rendezvous with his men back at the tavern. The door opened, and it was Louis with another man.

"Louis, when did you go back out? You were asleep when I came home a couple of hours ago." Gabriel grabbed his jacket off the chair.

"I woke up when you came in, thought I'd go back to sleep, but didn't. I decided to walk down to the docks. I'm glad I did. This is Steven Montoya, and he has information on where Edward England might be." Louis sat in one of the chairs in the room and motioned for Gabriel and Steven to do the same.

"Please Steven, tell me what information you know." Gabriel sat on a stool.

"My uncle has been friends with Mr. England for many years. They were both officers in the English Navy. He usually stays with him when he comes to Cape Verde." Steven sat back in his chair. "If you find him there, please don't start a gun battle. I don't want anything to happen to my uncle or his family."

"We'll wait for the right moment to flush him out. I only need my wife back." Gabriel stood up and paced the floor. "Where is this ranch?"

Steven gave him directions on how to locate the ranch and then left. Gabriel sent Louis to the tavern to get two guys and meet him at the livery. When they arrived, he had lined up four horses for them to use. He worried if they had enough men to overcome any resistance.

It was a couple of hour's ride through hills and rocks to the ranch which explained why many people in town hadn't seen him.

He speculated about what they might encounter when they made it to the ranch. The last hour, they rode in silence, not wanting anybody to hear them coming.

Chapter Twenty-Three

Olivia opened her eyes. It was the fourth night of sleeping in a comfortable bed. She still couldn't believe she'd been captured by pirates, then taken to a magnificent ranch near the ocean where she spent her days relaxing on the beach and learning how to paint.

Edward decided not to leave her on the ship with no one to watch over her. He had been buddies with the owner of the ranch, William Townsend, for years. Olivia could tell they had a great friendship. William's wife recently passed away, but they both treated Olivia with the utmost respect. Sometimes she forgot she was a prisoner. Then she remembered the day Manuel had been shot and a wave of sadness and grief hit her.

When Gabriel and his family received the news, they'd be devastated. She wondered what Gabriel was doing at this very moment. Did he care that she left to return to Florida? Had he moved forward with plans to marry Elisabeth? Her heart ached at those thoughts.

She pulled back the blankets and got out of bed. The view outside the window included palm trees and a florescent teal-colored ocean. The beaches here were every bit as beautiful as Florida, only in a different way. She decided to take a walk later to have something to do.

William gave her a couple of dresses from his wife and they fit perfectly. The one she had been wearing on the ship was beyond dirty. How do these people live without a washer and dryer? I guess you don't miss something you've never experienced. The weight of the gowns became too much at times. Obviously, men had designed them, women wouldn't want to put themselves through misery every day?

After fixing her hair, she went to the dining room. Both Edward and William stood when she walked in.

"You look lovely in that dress, Olivia. Marie would be pleased that someone is getting some use from it." William smiled.

"Thank you, William." Olivia sat across the table from them. "I appreciate you letting me have them."

"My wife would want me to give them all away, but I'm not ready to part with that many. I miss her so much. The days are long without her here. I've considered moving back to England. I have family there." William took a bite of eggs.

Edward sat back in his chair. "That is a great idea."

"I'd hoped to have you nearby and believe you should go back to England. It's time you give up your life as a pirate. Your wife needs you near." William handed a plate of biscuits to Olivia.

"I wish I could, but I need the money for her care. I can't believe that blasted crewman shot and killed the King of Spain's son. Why was he so stupid? He couldn't live after such a poor decision. I am certain if the King finds out he'll hold me responsible. I don't know how I'd make amends for this. I'll be one of the most hunted men alive." Edward buttered his biscuit.

"I'd say you're in a bit of jam. You should've been

wiser in choosing your crewmen." William looked at Olivia. "I'm sorry, Olivia. We should be more considerate. I understand your sister hoped to marry the King's son."

"It will be extremely hard for her. Would it be okay if I go down to the beach? I'd like to clear my thoughts and listen to the ocean." Olivia stood up.

"That should be fine. It's our private beach, so you should be alone. I'll have Rosie go with you. I might even be down in a while to paint, but of course, this is all up to you, Edward."

"If you see no risk, then I agree." Both men stood as Olivia left the room.

She went upstairs to grab a shawl and a sketch pad. Well, that's what she'd call it. She needed to pander to William and his love of art.

She strolled to the beach with Rosie beside her and they sat in the sand under a palm tree. Olivia guessed the temperature to be in the seventies with a light offshore breeze. While she rested, she considered how things had changed concerning her love of God. The last few days off of the ship had given her time to focus on all that took place. God spoke to her in the quiet moments. She'd hear the words, everything will be ok, in her head and then peace would cover her. She didn't understand why, but she knew He loved her. She realized He hadn't been indifferent or uncaring, and His answer may have been different from what she expected it should be, but He made good from the bad. He protected her.

Olivia wanted to ask Gabriel a lot of questions but didn't know if they'd ever see each other again. Honestly, who knows what these men might do to her? They appeared to be nice and civilized, but if it came down to their life or hers, she didn't stand a chance.

She picked up the sketch pad and drew the contours of the waves. If only she could make them look as magical as they do with her eyes. She breathed in deep as if to hold the smells, sights, and noises locked in her memory.

The cracking of a tree branch startled her. She heard loud noises, like an animal in the underbrush. *Maybe I should hide behind a bush or something.* Looking through the trees, she saw horses and riders heading her way.

"Olivia, we need to run to the house," Rosie yelled.

Olivia forgot Rosie came with her, she'd been so consumed in her thoughts. Her heart picked up its beat as she pulled up her skirts and ran toward the house.

Chapter Twenty-Four

Two women were running from the beach toward the ranch house. One had the same hair color as Olivia's. Was it her? "Olivia!" Gabriel yelled.

The woman kept moving. Did she hear him?

"Olivia!" He yelled as loud as he could. This time she stopped, then looked back. She held her hand over her eyes, protecting them from the sun while she stared at them.

Louis hollered. "Olivia, it's us."

Olivia started sprinting toward them, but the other woman caught up and grabbed her arm. She was taller and Olivia struggled to pull away. Edward and William rushed out of the house. Two men came from around the side of the house.

As they galloped closer, one of the guys yelled for them to stop. Gabriel and his men slowed their horses to a trot and then a complete halt. They were near enough to recognize that it was Olivia. He was so glad to see her. He'd feared she'd be gone forever. He wasn't going to let these guys hurt her.

"I said you have come close enough! Edward

pointed his pistol at them. Stop right there! Advance no further!" Edward told Rosie to take Olivia inside.

"I am not going inside, one of those men is my husband," Olivia screamed.

"You said your husband was on his way to Florida. I thought there was more to your story." Edward glanced at Olivia.

"I demand that you let my wife go." Gabriel and his men had drawn their pistols as well. The situation had developed into a standoff.

"Olivia is not going anywhere with you. She wants to go to Florida and I'm taking her there." Edward took Olivia's arm and ordered Rosie inside.

"You'll become a wanted man by the King of Spain if you push this matter any further. I'm his son, Captain Gabriel Rodriquez."

"I'm already on that list, so I haven't much to lose. However, you have a lot to lose." Edward grabbed Olivia, pulling her in front of him. "I don't want to hurt her, but I have to think of myself and my family first."

"Edward, what are you doing?" William interjected. "This will not get you anywhere." William stepped past Edward toward Gabriel. "If I may, I wish to speak on my friend's behalf.

"William, you have nothing to do with this, it would be best for you to go inside. He's not going to negotiate once he knows the truth." Edward moved in front of William.

"What truth? Do you mean the truth that one of your crew murdered my brother? The truth that you and your pirates attacked and killed many of the crewmen aboard my brother's ship, then set it ablaze, leaving the few remaining men to drown or burn? That's a pretty dark truth and one that causes my blood to boil."

"Gabriel, he didn't want Manuel killed. One of his men went rogue and shot him against orders not to. But he spared me and has treated me with kindness and respect. What's done is done. Can't we agree that we all go our separate ways before someone else is killed?" Olivia's eyes were pleading with everyone there.

"He was just threatening to kill you, Olivia. Do you think my father won't want revenge against a lunatic pirate for killing his son, his fellow countrymen, and burning one of Spain's ships? The king might be lenient and sentence him to life in prison instead of hanging if he turns himself in. Otherwise, I would rather take care of this right now."

"Gabriel, how's this going to end? There are weapons drawn on both sides. Do you wish to see me or Louis killed in a gun battle?" Olivia nervously wiped her brow.

William stepped back in front of Edward. "She's right, Edward. Why, would you do this?"

"Move out of the way, William! They will shoot us." Edward tried to shove William to the side, but in so doing it gave Olivia the chance she needed to escape Edward's grasp and run.

Just like that, Edward had lost his only advantage… Olivia. But weapons remained drawn.

Olivia climbed onto the back of Louis' horse. "What would be best for everybody right now is if we call this a draw. Nobody needs to be killed."

Gabriel had taken back what he came for, Olivia. He realized she was right. He didn't want to chance her being shot just because he wanted revenge against Edward. Also, there was the nephew in town who had told Gabriel about his uncle and the pirate being friends, and he'd promised to not get William killed. They'd ride out of here with his wife and take up this fight again at a later date.

"You're outnumbered, Edward, four to three. Your only advantage was having my wife in your possession. If you recognize what's best for you and your friend William right now, you'll do nothing as we ride off."

Edward scowled. "You caught me off guard, Captain Rodriquez. Be assured we'll meet again under different terms."

Chapter Twenty-Five

Gabriel paced the cabin floor while Olivia sat on the bed. They hadn't spoken all the way to the ship. Louis asked many questions about how she had been treated until they got onboard.

"Why would that ruthless pirate treat you differently than others he has victimized?" Gabriel hit his fist on the desk in his room. "I've racked my brain and can't come up with a reason."

"Gabriel, I'm telling you the truth, he treated me like I was his sister. He didn't do anything to me. It does seem unexplainable, considering what you've told me about him in the last few minutes. There is no explanation. That's why I believe it was God who protected me." Olivia looked up at him with unshed tears in her eyes.

"What? Since when do you believe in God? You've said He doesn't exist, or He doesn't care. Why would He protect you over my brother, a successor to the throne of Spain? You don't even belong here." Gabriel spat on the floor. "You were right, I should've let you stay in your time."

"Why are you acting this way, Gabriel?" Olivia asked as tears ran down her face. "This is not the man I married."

"Why am I acting this way? First, my wife leaves with my brother. Then, I find out Manuel is dead and my wife has been captured by one of the most notorious pirates ever to sail the seas. I've tried to please God. So, either God doesn't care, or I haven't done enough." Gabriel kicked a boot across the floor.

"You kissed Elisabeth. I went in search of her as she left the room where Francesca played the piano. I ended up on a balcony overlooking the gardens and spotted a couple standing close together in the sunset. At first, I thought how romantic, and then I realized it was you and her. I turned my head away for a second to decide if I should go down and interrupt and when I glanced back the two of you were kissing.

After everything you've said to me about honoring our marriage commitment, and after all we've been through together, you went from protecting my honor to betraying it. How could you! Maybe you've answered your questions. Olivia stood up. "Maybe God doesn't honor a man's prayers when he's not being faithful to his wife."

"That's funny, you calling me unfaithful. The woman who flirted with my brother every chance she got. The woman who, according to the palace servants, was sobbing her eyes out in his arms and was the reason he hastily fled with her on his ship. What were the two of you doing aboard the vessel? If he hadn't left so swiftly, he'd probably still be alive because his route wouldn't have crossed Edward England." Gabriel looked away. "For your information, I was not kissing her. She'd forced her mouth on mine. I tried to twist away, but she grabbed my head forcefully with both hands, preventing me from doing so. I could have easily pushed her off of me but was afraid I'd cause her to fall and be injured. I didn't want to be accused of hurting a woman.

"Would've served her right. I did nothing on the ship with Manuel. How dare you accuse me of that, nor did I flirt with him. I didn't spend any time with him on the boat. He stayed away from me once I said I wanted to return to Spain. I threw up all the time and when I wasn't puking, I could hardly lift my head as I was so dizzy.

The only person I saw was the cabin boy who emptied my buckets and brought me some food and water. A few days in, I asked Manuel to take me back to Spain, but he refused. I realized I was wrong to have left so suddenly, and that I should have spoken to you first.

I cried out to God when we were under attack by the pirates, and he spared my life. He also healed me from my nausea and dizziness. You can place the blame for his death on me. I understand why you believe I am at fault. I have thought the same.

I did not want Manuel to be beaten and shot. I can't even talk about how horrific it was. When I glanced at his lifeless body on the floor, it broke my heart. I wept and screamed while that disgusting pirate threatened to kill me. He would've if Edward hadn't walked through the door. The flashbacks of that moment are awful. I've spent hours thinking about you, and your parents, knowing how devastating this will be." Olivia bent over sobbing. "I never asked for any of this."

"Neither did I." Gabriel opened the door of the cabin and slammed it as he walked out.

He hated how he was acting. He didn't recognize the person who said those things to Olivia.

As he got on deck, Louis walked toward him. "You just got Olivia back, yet you look angry, or is it sad? This should be the best day of your life." Louis followed Gabriel to the boat's railing.

"Both. I said things I never should've, although I want to believe I'm justified. It would be a lie. I don't know who I am. It's as if someone else is talking and I'm observing." Gabriel kept his face turned out toward the sea.

"I know what the problem is, but do you want to hear it? Are you ready to set sail?" Louis asked.

"I am. Let's go home. Although, I'm not ready to tell my parents their son is gone. What is my problem, Louis?" Gabriel finally swung around.

"You've shut God out of your life and you're blaming Him for choices that were not His. You have to forgive, Gabriel. This is not Olivia's or God's fault. Manuel chose to leave early to try to take your wife from you. The man who shot him made a choice. It was not fair, but God allows each of us to make our own decisions whether they're good or evil. It's easy to love and trust God when everything is going great, but not when someone's wrong choices bring devastation to our lives. Getting quiet and spending some time in prayer would be beneficial for you." Louis grasped his shoulder. "I will instruct the men to prepare to sail."

Chapter Twenty-Six

"Captain! Pirate ship off the starboard quarter."

Loud blasts filled the air. Wood shards flew in every direction as a direct hit ripped a hole in the deck.

"We're under attack. Tighten the sails. Prepare to return fire." Shouts from the crew echoed through the air.

Olivia screamed as another and more powerful impact caused the ship to rock violently. *Not again.*

She made her way to the deck as a cannonball flew across the bow, blasting through the railing. She screamed again.

Gabriel ran to her and yelled. "Go back to the cabin. It's safer there than here. Edward threatened to meet us again, and here he is."

"I need to stay out here." Olivia glared at Gabriel.

"Then go over by the doors and pray, God seems to be answering your prayers. We need all the help we can get. We're sitting ducks out here."

"I thought you didn't believe in prayer." Olivia challenged.

"I'm rethinking my stance. Besides, it can't do any harm." He said as he turned and ran toward Louis.

Olivia prayed. The sails were up, yet the ship barely

moved. They were going upwind, requiring them to tack. Edward's ship had been equipped with fore-and-aft sails, allowing his boat to sail upwind at a greater rate of speed, and he was catching them. But why had they ceased firing their cannons?

The thoughts came too soon, as another cannonball landed in the water, just missing the stern. A gust of wind came out of nowhere and filled the sails as they tacked port-side. The vessel picked up momentum, allowing Gabriel to call for a maneuver to swing the ship around, facing their attacker. They were now downwind, and the sails snapped taut as they caught the swiftly moving breeze. They quickly moved forward, toward Edward's boat at a high rate of speed.

A crewman bellowed. "Ship's coming upon us, Captain."

"Cannons at the ready."

"Fire!" Gabriel yelled.

Loud booms echoed through her ears as the cannons fired.

"We took out a forward mast and sail," Gabriel yelled.

"That should slow them down a bit." Louis hollered.

A cannonball tore through the edge of the deck and hull, sending wood fragments flying. A few men screamed out in pain, causing her to cover her ears.

A few of the crewmen yelled. "Men down, the Captain's been hit."

Olivia saw Gabriel lying on the deck, blood oozing from a tear in his jacket. She ran over to him. "Are you alright?"

"I'll be fine, it's only a scratch. Now get below deck, you're not safe out here."

"Cannons ready, Captain," Louis yelled.

"Then fire!" Gabriel struggled to sit up.

Olivia covered her ears as the cannons rang out again. Seconds later, a cheer burst forth from the men on deck. She looked to see the mainsail tumbling over, hanging half off Edward's ship.

"She's dead in the water, Captain. You have some mighty fine marksmen with those cannons." Louis grinned.

"Let's finish em off! Cannons ready!" Gabriel shouted as he got back on his feet.

"Aye, Sir."

"Fire!" Gabriel commanded.

Two cannonballs struck the side of Edwards's vessel, just above the water line, leaving a gaping hole. Seawater rushed into the hull of the ship, causing it to list. Within minutes, the boat rolled over, throwing the crew on deck overboard.

"Captain, should we capture them or let them meet their fate?" A crewman yelled.

"We've done what we came to do. Back to Spain!"

The men whooped in celebration.

Louis put his arm around Gabriel. "Let's get you to your cabin and check that scratch."

Gabriel laid down on the bed in his cabin. Olivia helped him take his jacket and shirt off.

A crewman who also acted as the ship's doctor, followed them into the room. "It's gonna need a few stitches, that's a pretty nasty wound. You're fortunate, it barely missed an artery. You'll have a large scar, but should be fine as long as the wound is kept clean."

The doctor washed the wound thoroughly before sewing it up and dressing it.

Gabriel removed the towel from his mouth he had used to bite down on, sweat ran in a stream down his face. "Treating the injury hurts worse than getting it, Doc."

Olivia breathed a sigh of relief. Her heart rate returned to normal. She was still mad at Gabriel over the way he talked to her, accusing her of a dalliance with Manuel. She left the cabin and walked out into the sunshine. She wanted to see if she could help the doctor with any men who were wounded. There were quite a few injuries, but nothing life-threatening.

There was damage to the ship, but in places that didn't affect the boat's seaworthiness. They should be able to get back to Spain without a problem, at least that's what the men were saying.

Olivia had mixed emotions. Gabriel had calmed down, but she felt uncertain. She had no choice but to go back as her cousin Gregory mentioned in his letter he didn't know if she'd be able to return to her time again from the Florida beach. She may be living in the eighteenth century on her own. Olivia had been alone most of her life. She would do it, there wasn't another choice.

I'll be with you, Olivia.

Was that God speaking to her? With everything that happened since going back in time, finding out Jesus loved her and did care was worth it all. She leaned over the railing, looking up at the sky as the sea breeze and salt spray showered her face. She was alive and heading back to Spain. The horror of the last few weeks was over.

Chapter Twenty-Seven

Gabriel's injured arm throbbed. It'd been two days since he was wounded. Louis had several hours talking with him concerning the grief he was going through over Manuel's death. Gabriel expressed resentment at God, and Louis told him God could handle his anger. Louis prayed with him numerous times, asking God for clarity in everything that had transpired, but it would take him a while to work through all these emotions.

He hadn't seen or spoken with Olivia the past two days. Because of his injury and everything he was dealing with, he'd stayed in his cabin and instructed his first mate to captain the ship. He needed to talk to her, and since she was sleeping in the room next to his, there was no better moment than now. When the cabin boy came in, he asked him to tell her he wanted to see her.

A tap sounded on his door a few minutes later.

"Come in."

Olivia entered his room and Gabriel drank in the sight of her. He'd missed her dearly and realized his anguish over the passing of his brother caused him to lash out at her. She stood in front of him, waiting.

"I need to start by saying I'm sorry, Olivia. I shouldn't have said the words I did to you. I was furious at God, grieving my brother and scared to death I would find you dead. Louis and I have talked, and he's helped me understand how unfair I've been and how important you are to me. I let my emotions get the best of me, and I took it out on you, and again I'm sorry."

"You weren't nice. It hurt deeply to hear you blame me for Manuel's death. I don't understand why I survived, and he didn't." Tears ran down Olivia's face.

"I'm so thankful you survived. I don't know how I could've said those words to you. It wasn't your fault. I was hurting and lashed out from that place. It was wrong." Gabriel stood and reached for her hand. He drew her close and hugged her with his good arm, her head resting on his chest. "I love you, Olivia. I never wanted to marry Elisabeth, and I certainly never wanted her to kiss me.

I was devastated, thinking that I might never see you again. I couldn't understand why you'd leave with Manuel without speaking to me. We're meant to be together, whether in this year or yours. After we get to Spain and have time to grieve with my family over Manuel's death, I will take you back to Florida. If we travel into your age, so be it. I need you to be happy."

"Chances are we won't be able to go forward in time again. I received a mysterious letter from someone who knows our secret. It's a long story." Olivia stared into his eyes. "I love you too, and I'm sorry, I should've talked to you."

Gabriel had enough conversation. He put his finger over her lips, then kissed them long and tenderly. He moved the hair back off the side of her face with his nose, as he ran a string of kisses down onto her neck. He then paused to gaze into her eyes. What he saw there reassured him. "God has blessed us even in these crazy and unexplainable circumstances. I want to hear about the letter, but now is not the time.

"What will we do when we get back, Gabriel? I doubt if your parents ever accept me." Olivia started to ask more questions, but he stopped her with a brief kiss.

Gabriel smiled. "I need to take you away from everybody for a while so we can begin our marriage anew. This time, the way it should be. Two people in love and planning their lives. I was thinking of when we will start a family. I want lots of children, Olivia."

Olivia blushed. "I'm not that young, so we better have them quickly."

"A little girl who looks like her mommy would make my heart full." Gabriel kissed her again. "You are way more valuable than all that we lost in Florida. I believe God has an important plan for us."

"I flew to Florida searching for lost treasure from your ships, and found you, a three-hundred-year-old man." Olivia laughed as she kissed him.

"Yes, you're married to a very old man. No matter what happens, I am not going to let go of you, Olivia." Gabriel hugged her.

"I'll hold you to that Captain Gabriel Matias Rodriquez," Olivia said, wrapping her arms around his neck.

He'd be lying if he didn't admit to having uneasiness about their future, but for now, he was thankful for the present.

The End

Darlia loves living in Western Colorado with her husband, Ken. Their lives have been blessed with six children and four grandchildren.

Darlia is a multi-published author in both fiction and non-fiction. She writes Inspirational Romance in many genres.

To find out more visit her on:

https://amazon.com/author/darliasawyer

https://www.facebook.com/DarliaSawyerAuthor

https://www.instagram.com/darliasawyer

https://www.goodreads.com/author/show/16670538.Darlia_Sawyer

(2) Pinterest

Thank you for reading Treasure Beyond Time. I hope you enjoyed it. I plan on making this story into a series. I'm not ready to say good-bye to Olivia and Gabriel yet. In the meantime I would love for you to check out my other novellas. Each book is steeped in suspense, mystery and, of course, romance.

Inspirational Historical Romance (1800's)

Also by Darlia Sawyer
Texas Orphan Train Series
Book One: A Home for Her Heart
Blurb:

Thrown out on the streets of New York City, and doubting God's existence, Anna Wilson accepts a job at the Children's Aid Society. As an agent for the Society, she travels the west on trains full of orphans in search of families and homes. Because of Anna's personal heartache and loss, she devotes herself to placing the children in only the very best families.

After an embarrassing introduction to Texas cattle rancher, Joshua Brown, a widower, Anna makes a surprise visit to his ranch. Their encounter throws them into a series of events which neither one was ready for. Can their mutual attraction overcome the differences and past heartbreaks as they fight to save the children in their care? One man bent on revenge could destroy it all.

Texas Orphan Train Series
Book Two: A Healing Heart
Burb:
Saving an outlaw's life on her way to Texas hadn't been part of Sophie Knowles plans. It pushed her from wanting to be a doctor to becoming the first female doctor in the small town of Nacogdoches. Acceptance won't come easy, but Sophie's determination keeps her moving forward.

Wesley Johnson can't shake the guilt from an apartment building fire which left him and his infant sister, Katie, orphaned in New York City. After living in an orphanage, at fifteen he flees his past looking to earn a better life for them both. After seven years and feeling like a failure, he contacts the orphanage only to find out Katie is on an orphan train heading west.

Luke Nelson had proven himself a valuable foreman on Joshua Brown's ranch. His luck with women left him disheartened. Maybe he was meant to be alone.

A gang of cattle rustlers threatens their tiny town, throwing their lives into a passionate pursuit of justice. Will the gang's ruthlessness destroy all they hold dear?

Can Sophie prove her ability under pressure while Luke and Wesley search for the acceptance and healing their hearts crave?

Texas Orphan Train Series
Book Three: A Captive Heart

Blurb:
Private Investigator, Shane Wyatt, has endangered the lives of everyone he holds dear. When given the opportunity to right his wrongs, Shane believes his luck has turned.

Taken captive to pay a man's gambling debt, Ella Brown finds herself face to face with a past she's never known. After Shane saves her life, Ella begins to wonder if his bizarre tale might be true.

Neither of them can foresee where this adventure will take them as it forces them into a battle between greed and forgiveness. Ella will have to abandon the story she's believed her whole life in order to find the truth.

Stand Alone

Book One: A Place of Grace
Blurb:
Drake West loves his wife, Noel. The responsibilities of being sheriff leave him little time for her and cause them to drift apart. A rash of arson and murders entwine him in a plot where the price of failure is everything that matters.

Noel West is frustrated with being alone and too accepting of Banker Charles Steele's flirtations. He plays on Noel's loneliness and vulnerability. She's naïve to who he really is as he pulls her into a world of deception and lies.

Charles Steele is obsessed with the sheriff's wife. He has secrets which will tear the town apart and prove he's not the upstanding citizen he claims to be.

In a moment of certain death and with their relationship in peril, could a Christmas miracle save them?

Stand Alone

Early 1900's England

Book One: Frayed Dreams
Blurb:
Grace Bolling grew up loved and sheltered in the small fishing parish of Bridlington, on the coast of England. In the fall of 1910, her life changed dramatically the day her parents sent her to York, to work as a seamstress for her aunt, a well-renowned dressmaker for the nobility.

Lord William Stanley, second in line to inherit the family's estate, has always been the good son. Yet never good enough for his father. Williams's father, Earl Richard doesn't accept his son's defiance in not honoring a marriage arranged by Lady Elisabeth Ashfield's parents. Is William willing to reject the expectations of his family to find companionship in the blue eyes of a seamstress?

Grace is swept away by the handsome Lord and unsure of where it might lead. Their attraction draws unwanted attention from those with a different agenda for their lives. Will threats of violence and intimidation keep Grace from finding love with a man she can never have?

Inspirational Contemporary Romance

Book One: Burning Love
Blurb:
Orphaned at seven because of her mother's suicide and her father's abandonment, Emily Hayes, finds love in the arms of her grandmother, Barbara Stuart, an avid Elvis fan.

Barbara trusts almost every man she meets. Emily has only known one man she could trust. However, a chance encounter at a concert with a handsome cowboy and his grandfather may change their perspectives.

Luke Morgan is a rancher and volunteer fireman. Luke relies on only one person in his life, himself, and he doesn't see that changing. His grandfather, John Morgan, thrilled audiences as an Elvis impersonator in his youth. But after his wife's death, he struggles to find happiness.

Neither Luke nor Emily want to be in a relationship, but their grandparents budding friendship keeps bringing them together. A mutual attraction blossoms between them, but will ties to their pasts pose an obstacle to their future?

Emily and Luke struggle to let go of the forces which are crippling their emotions as their grandparents stand with them. Will they embrace the peace and hope of a better life that comes from being tried by fire?

Enjoy Chapter One of: A Home for Her Heart

1891

Chapter One

Tears spilled down Ella's cheeks as Anna Wilson helped her step off the orphan train in Longview, Texas. She embraced the twelve-year-old girl. "What's wrong, Ella? Are you tired? I would understand if you were. We've traveled to so many towns in the last several weeks."

Ella wiped tears from her eyes. "No one wants me."

"I'm trying my best to find homes for each of you. You all deserve to have the love of a family." Anna hugged the six children in her care. "I have a good feeling about today. The last agent said several families' were waiting for the next orphan train."

Anna noticed Ella's flushed cheeks "Ella, you look warm. Are you running a temperature?"

"I don't think so." Ella pulled at the front of her dress. "It's hot."

"This Texas humidity is suffocating." Anna laid her hand on Ella's forehead. "You're not running a temperature. I hope the people today understand what gifts each of you are. We're late, let's go find the opera house."

Anna followed the six children along the wooden sidewalk. Ella's red curls bounced with each step she took. Dust engulfed them from the passing horses and wagons. Michael coughed. *Did anyone ever get used to all this dirt?* Anna understood now why they covered the streets in New York with brick. It made walking so much easier. They passed by a bakery and the aroma of homemade bread made Anna's mouth water.

"I'm hungry. Can we buy sweet rolls, Miss Wilson?" Sam asked.

"I wish we had time. They smell wonderful." Anna spotted the opera house across the street. "We're almost there."

Anna opened the door of a two-story brick building and they walked in. Their train had arrived an hour late, and there were around twenty people waiting for them. There were more women than men sitting in groups and talking. A middle-aged man in a black suit came toward them.

"Welcome. I'm Pastor Williams and we've been expecting you." He held his hand out to Anna. "Did everyone have a pleasant trip?" He didn't wait for the children to respond. He asked Anna. "Are you comfortable introducing yourself?"

She shook his hand. "Yes to both questions and thank you. Children, please go sit in the chairs they've set out on stage."

Anna followed the children down the aisle, admiring the stained-glass windows of the Longview Opera House. There were four long windows on each side, and they cast shades of yellow, red, green and blue on the wooden floor in a kaleidoscope of colors. Each window depicted a scene from a famous play. It reminded Anna of the church her parents attended when she was a little girl. She hadn't been to church since then. Grief caught Anna by surprise and she had a difficult time holding back tears. Her parents had died eight years ago.

Her heart broke for each child on stage. Most of them had never known their parents, and the rest had lost theirs at a young age. The orphanage had provided the girls with white dresses, stockings, shoes and a bow. The four boys had on white shirts, jackets, knee pants, hats, socks and shoes. They looked adorable. Their sole possessions included one more outfit and a Bible.

Anna stepped to the front of the stage. She no longer got nervous speaking in front of people. Her concern for the children pushed her to overcome the anxiousness she used to feel.

"I want to thank everyone for coming. My name is Anna Wilson. I am an agent for the Children's Aid Society in New York City. We have traveled many miles to find families who will love these children. I care about each of them."

"They listen well and are considerate and loving. In the past, many people thought it appropriate to treat orphans as servants. I won't allow this." Anna glared at the audience. "I hope you'll love them as your own. Most of them were living on the streets before someone took them to the Children's Aid Society. They'd lost one or both parents and often their siblings. Their lives have been filled with difficulties and sorrow. My hope is you'll find it a privilege to provide a home for them. In return they'll show you how much it means to be a part of your family."

"When I finish speaking, I hope you'll talk with each child. I have a few rules," Anna studied the crowd. "I don't allow anyone to touch their muscles or look at their teeth. They're all healthy. Agents used to allow this, but I won't. They need respect. If you're interested in a child, I'll check with Longview's community leaders to find out if they believe your family would provide a good home. The children must feel comfortable around you, so I'll watch how you communicate and connect with them." She cleared her throat. "Could we get a drink of water? We had a long train ride and we're not used to this heat."

Pastor Williams left and returned with a bucket of water and a ladle.

"Thank you." Anna let the children drink first. She wished they had ice for the warm

water, but it eased her parched throat.

"I'd like to introduce everyone. Children, please step forward when I say your name. First is Sam Foster, he's twelve." A lanky brown haired boy took his place by Anna. "A family in Opelousas, Louisiana took his younger brother Ben. They didn't have room for both boys. Sam has Ben's address so he can write to him. He wants to visit him one day. Their parents died in a factory fire. When Sam was eight and Ben was five, someone found them on the streets and brought them to the orphanage."

"Next is Ella Murphey, she's twelve." Ella stood next to Sam. She was taller than him and her red curls stuck out in every direction. Her cheeks grew pink which caused her freckles to appear darker. "Ella helps with the little ones. I don't know what I would've done without her. She doesn't remember her family. Her father brought her to the orphanage when she was three."

"Then we have Matthew, he's ten." He tried to go on the opposite side of Miss Wilson but Ella grabbed his arm and pulled him beside her. Matthew frowned at Ella but recovered quickly and turned toward the audience and smiled, causing dimples to appear in his chubby cheeks. "His parents and siblings died from typhoid. A couple found him huddled in a corner of the apartment building they'd lived in and took him to the orphanage."

Anna motioned to the small blonde-haired girl to stand next to her. "Laura is eight. When her parents didn't return from a voyage to England, her grandmother cared for her. No one ever heard what happened to her parents. When her grandmother died Laura was only four. A family friend brought her to the orphanage."

"Last are five-year-old twins, Scott and Michael." They ran next to Laura. Each brother a mirror image of the other, black short hair, bright blue eyes and two missing top teeth. "If you're thinking about taking them, I hope you'll take both. Twins have a special connection. Their mother left them on the steps of the orphanage when they were babies. She'd pinned a note stating their names, and that she had no other choice. Thank you children, you can sit down. Does anyone have questions before you talk with them?" Anna watched a man get up and walk out. He wore torn jean overalls, and a ripped shirt. She wondered how often he bathed as there were dirt smudges across his face.

A woman with thick glasses stood up as she squinted at Anna. "If you're not married can you care for a child?"

Anna scanned the crowd. She guessed most of them to be in their late twenties or early thirties, including the woman asking the question. "We prefer you're married, but if you want to care for a child, we're willing to let you try."

A man in a gray vest, jacket, matching trousers and black top hat stood, "Do you check on each child after they go with a family? What if a child is unhappy and doesn't want to stay in your home? Or if the families realize they can't care for them, how would you resolve it?"

"Yes, agents check on the children each time they bring new orphans. I'll be here for two weeks to make sure they're adjusting well and to make sure children from previous orphan trains are doing well. The agent after me should do the same. If a child is unhappy, we find another family for them. If we can't, we take them back to the Children's Aid Society in New York City. Children have run away from homes, and we've never heard from them again. We often learn afterward that those children were being physically or emotionally mistreated." Anna patted Scott's shoulder as he hopped from one foot to the other.

An older woman in the back row covered her mouth with her gloved hand. "Oh my, who would do such awful things?"

"Sometimes a neighbor or family member will do things in the privacy of their home you'd never imagine. I hope if you notice or hear something bad happening in a family, you'll report it. I'm glad most problems we have aren't so awful and are easily worked out." Anna paused and tucked a few loose strands of her toffee brown hair behind her ear. "Anyone else?" No one spoke. "If you come up with other questions, I'd love to answer them. Thank you for coming."

Anna paced the stage as people came to talk with the children. It'd be difficult to let any of the children go. She'd come to love them. She walked over and stood in front of the curtain on the right side of the stage. She needed to get her emotions under control. Anna heard whispering behind her.

"Mary, what about the two girls?" A hoarse voice asked.

Anna noticed a hole in the curtain. She could see two older women through it.

"I'm not sure about the little girl, Bertha. The taller girl with red hair appears adequate." Mary glanced at the girls. "No one is saying anything to her, so you might be her only opportunity."

"I don't have time for nonsense. I need someone to do the housework I can no longer do. My health makes it difficult for me. I'm too old to take care of a child." Bertha sat in a wooden chair. It groaned and creaked beneath her. "She would have to follow my rules."

"Bertha, if she's in school, she can only help you in the evenings. And all children misbehave. I wonder if you have sufficient patience to have a child around, even an older one. Maybe this isn't the best solution for you." Mary sat next to her, clutching a big bag to her bosom.

"She doesn't need more school. She'll get real life experience taking care of a home. If she marries, she will need to know household management." Bertha scooted back in her chair, a snap caused her to stand abruptly, as the chair broke into pieces all over the floor. "They sure don't make chairs like they used to."

Anna had heard enough. She went around the curtain. "I overheard your conversation, and I won't let Ella leave with you. As I expressed in my introduction, they're not servants. They need love and a family. Ella is a lovely and helpful girl. She deserves more than someone who wants a housekeeper. You should both leave."

"Of all the nerve. Mary, let's go." Bertha's face turned red. "The mayor will hear about this. I wanted to help that child, and this is how I'm treated." Bertha waddled down the stairs, huffing and puffing her way through the people and out the door. Mary followed behind her.

Anna's heart raced as she walked back to the front of the stage. Her nails dug into her palms as she clenched her hands into fists. Her cheeks were on fire and she knew her face was red. *I can't believe how selfish people are. Ella deserves a real family.*

The well-dressed man who had asked the questions earlier approached Anna. He was holding hands with an attractive women. "Miss Wilson, my name is Thomas Gage, and this is my wife, Emma." He shook Anna's hand. "We're interested in providing a home for the twins. In our five years of marriage we haven't been blessed with children. Our home is nice and we have four bedrooms. I'm the town doctor and my wife would stay with them."

Anna drew a deep breath. "I appreciate you wanting to provide a home for them but are you aware of how rambunctious two little boys can be? They might destroy something valuable. If you had children of your own, would you still want the twins? Or would they be a burden to you?" Anna glared at Emma.

"Oh no, Miss Wilson, we'd think of the boys as ours." Mrs. Gage paused. "They'd be the older siblings to any child we might have. Once you give a child your heart, you wouldn't take it back. I assure you, God gives us enough love for everyone in our lives." She clutched her husband's hand as if clinging to a lifeline.

"I wonder if God bothers with such matters. He allowed their parents to give them away." Anna took a few deep breaths, to calm herself down. "I'm sorry if I sound cynical. Before I came over here, I overheard a conversation which upset me. My recommendation would be to take Michael and Scott for two hours today. When you're done, bring them to our hotel and you can do the same for the next few days. You could increase the time you have them each day. As long as everything goes well for the twins and both of you, we'll talk about a permanent arrangement." Anna smiled.

Mrs. Gage's expression softened. "Oh, what a wonderful idea. It'd give us time to get our home prepared." She glanced up at her husband. "What do you think, Thomas?"

"It's a good plan. We'll get to know them and they can decide if they want to live with us. Would it be all right if we took them to lunch and to our house to play? We have a large yard and a new furry puppy." Mr. Gage lifted his hat and wiped his forehead with a handkerchief.

"Let me talk with the boys. I'll be right back." Anna

walked over to Michael and Scott. "There's a couple who wishes to have lunch with you both. After eating they'll take you to their home to play with their new puppy for a while. Would you like to go with them?"

"Yes, Miss Wilson," Michael gave her a toothless smile.

Scott nodded. "I would love to play with a puppy."

"When you are through playing, they'll bring you to the hotel. You'll have lots of fun." Anna walked back with the boys to give the good news to Mr. and Mrs. Gage.

***

"Well girls, let's eat supper and find our hotel. Our luggage should be there." Anna took each girl by the hand. "I can't say I'm sorry the right family didn't come for you both. Now I have more time with you. We'll stay here for two weeks. Our next and last stop will be in Nacogdoches, Texas. I believe families are waiting there for both of you."

"It's all right Miss Wilson. No one wants me. They don't even speak to me. I'll go back to the orphanage with you." Ella wiped tears away.

"No one wants me either. They only take boys. I'm happy Sam, Matthew and the twins found families but why don't they like girls, Miss Wilson?" Laura looked up at Anna with her big blue eyes brimming with unshed tears. "Doesn't God want us to find a family?"

Anna's heart broke. The girls' lives had been full of disappointments. Every time she paraded them in front of families, their hopes were high they'd find a home. When they didn't, rejection and disappointment settled on them.

Anna understood their responses. She'd

experienced pain when the man she'd loved rejected her for someone else. At twenty-nine her prospects of finding love were slim. She resented the label of spinster, but it applied to her. Anna wanted a family but how could she ever trust a man with her heart again?

She needed a plan to take care of these precious girls. Ella's chances of someone wanting her for more than a housekeeper or nanny weren't good, as Anna had witnessed today. Laura wasn't as old, but girls weren't valued as highly as boys. The West needed laborers. Boys grew up and helped on the homesteads.

"Oh girls, you're beautiful. If the right family comes along, they'll love you as much as I do. I'm certain God wants you both to find families. Why wouldn't He? You're angels. After supper let's eat ice cream. It's been a long day and you both deserve a treat." Anna bent and wiped the tears away and kissed them on the cheek. "No more crying. It's time for fun."

Ella hugged Anna tight. "I wish we could stay with you, Miss Wilson."

"Me too." Laura joined in the hug.

"Me too." Anna whispered to herself.

***

The rocking rhythm of the train lolled Ella and Laura to sleep for most of the journey from Longview to Nacogdoches, Texas. Anna enjoyed looking out the window as forests and lakes sped by. She caught a whiff of coffee brewing in the dining car. Her stomach rumbled.

"Next stop Nacogdoches. Please prepare to disembark." The conductor announced.

Being an agent gave Anna the ability to travel and see places, but it didn't pay enough for her to live on her own. Maybe she should check into getting a teaching certificate and moving out West with the girls to teach.

Screeches and squeals from the train brakes startled Anna from her thoughts, and she looked outside at the depot coming into view.

Ella sat up, rubbing her eyes. "Are we there?"

"I believe so. We'll pick up our baggage and go to the hotel. I didn't know when we'd arrive when I sent out the telegram, so we won't be meeting with families until tomorrow." Anna stood. The girls followed her down the aisle.

"What a beautiful town." Anna glanced around at the small crowd as she stepped off the train. The smell of pine filled the air and evergreen trees stood as strong sentinels overlooking the area.

"It's pretty, Miss Wilson, so many trees. It's hot here too, but I like it. There's lots of shade." Ella stepped off the train.

Anna helped Laura down the steps. "Do you like it?"

"I do." Laura grabbed Ella's hand and smiled. "We'll meet our families here, Ella."

Ella stared at the ground. "You will, Laura."

"We need to get our luggage and find the hotel." Anna stepped backward and tripped over a satchel on the ground behind her. She tried regaining her balance, but instead strong arms wrapped around her waist. However, they didn't stop her fall. She landed on top of a muscular man.

"Oh my," Anna tried to push herself up. *Where should she place her hands so she wouldn't touch the man underneath her?* Her cheeks were on fire and people were starring.

"Miss Wilson, are you okay? That sure was funny," Ella giggled. "Grab my hands and I'll pull you up."

Anna made it to her feet and straightened her skirt. She turned around to thank the man who broke her fall. He wore jeans, brown cowboy boots and a white shirt. Dark brown hair waved from under his white cowboy hat. When she found the courage to look into his face, a pair of ice-blue eyes looked amused at her embarrassment. "I'm so sorry. I didn't check behind me before I backed up," she stammered. "Did I hurt you?"

"I'm fine, miss. Someone as slim as you wouldn't hurt me. I tried catching you but it didn't go as intended. Are you all right?" He held out his hand. "My name is Joshua."

Anna shook his hand. "I'm Anna Wilson and nothing is hurt, thanks to you. Glad you didn't hurt your head or break anything."

Joshua picked up the satchel. "It's dented. Is it yours?"

"It isn't. I wonder who'd sit a bag down and walk off?" Anna scanned the crowd, but no one rushed to claim the satchel. "I guess we should leave it, in case they come back. Do you know if they're unloading the luggage yet?"

Joshua sat the satchel on the ground. "We can find out. I need to get my mother's trunks. Follow me and I'll load your bags into your wagon."

"Oh, I wouldn't want to bother you with our bags. I'm sure you're busy, and we don't have a wagon. I'll hire someone to take our bags to the Grand Hotel." Anna took the girl's hands. "We'll follow you, though."

"It's no problem. I'll load your bags into my wagon and drop them off at the hotel. Which ones are yours? I'd offer you all a ride, but I'm out of room. My mother is coming to live with me and she brought enough trunks to fill two wagons. Which won't leave space for young ladies, sorry to say."

Anna tried to keep up with him. "Please don't bother about us. The girls and I like to walk. We'll get to see part of the town."

Joshua walked toward the men unloading luggage from the train to the wooden platform. He found his mother's trunks while Anna and the girls searched for theirs.

"We sat our luggage over there." Anna pointed to the bags. "Thank you again for helping us."

"You're welcome." Joshua smiled.

Anna's breath caught. Joshua had dimples, and his smile made her pulse pick up a beat or two. "Where is the Grand Hotel?"

"Turn right at the end of this street. It's three blocks down Main Street to the left. Have a good day ladies. It's nice to meet you." Joshua grabbed the bags.

"It was nice meeting you as well. Let's find the hotel, girls." Anna walked away but couldn't help taking one last glance at her rescuer. He was watching them. Their eyes met. Anna turned back around. *I'm sure he's married and has a family.*

She needed to accept her life. Her days would be filled with finding a home for the girls and checking on the children from previous orphan trains. Who had time for men, even the kind and handsome cowboy type men? He'd only end up breaking her heart.

www.ingramcontent.com/pod-product-compliance
Lightning Source LLC
LaVergne TN
LVHW012018060526
838201LV00061B/4355